Country Tales

Elizabeth Clark

Illustrated by Amanda Harvey

*Hodder
Children's
Books*

a division of Hodder Headline plc

Contents

The Old Woman who Lived in a Vinegar bottle

Once upon a time there was an Old Woman who lived in a Vinegar-bottle (she had a little ladder to go in and out by). She lived there for a great many years, but after a time she grew discontented (and wouldn't you – if you lived in a Vinegar-bottle?). And one day she began to grumble, and she grumbled so loud that a Fairy, who was passing by, heard her.

'Oh dear! Oh dear! Oh dear!' said the Old Woman. ' I *oughtn't* to live in a Vinegar-bottle. 'Tis a shame, so it is, 'tis a shame. I ought to live in a nice little white house, with pink curtains at the

1

windows and roses and honeysuckle growing over it, and there ought to be flowers and vegetables in the garden and a pig in a sty. So there ought. 'Tis a shame, so it is, '*tis* a shame.'

Well, the Fairy was sorry for her (and wouldn't you be sorry for a person who lived in a Vinegar-bottle?). And she said, 'Well, never you mind. But when you go to bed tonight, just you turn round three times, and when you wake up in the morning you'll see what you'll see!'

So the Old Woman went to bed in the Vinegar-bottle and she turned round three times. (I don't know how there was room to do it.) And when she woke up in the morning, she was in a little white bed in a room with pink curtains. And she jumped out of bed and ran across the room and pulled aside the pink curtains and looked out of the window. And it *was* a little white house, with roses and honeysuckle, and there was a garden with flowers and vegetables, and she could hear a *pig* – grunting in the sty!

Well, the Old Woman was pleased. But she never *thought* to say 'Thank you' to the Fairy.

Well, the Fairy she went East and she went West, and she went North and she went South;

and one day she came back to where the Old Woman was living in the little white house with pink curtains at the windows, and roses and honeysuckle – and flowers and vegetables in the garden – and the pig in the sty. And the Fairy said to herself, 'I'll just go and take a look at her. She *will* be pleased.'

But do you know, as the Fairy passed by the Old Woman's window, she could hear the Old Woman talking to herself, and *what* do you think she was saying? 'Oh! 'tis a shame,' said the Old Woman, ' 'tis a shame. So it is, '*tis* a shame. Why should I live in a pokey little cottage? Other folks live in little red brick houses on the edge of the town where they can watch who goes by to market. Why shouldn't *I* live in a little red brick house on the edge of town and see the folks going by to market? And I'm getting too old to do my own work. I ought to have a little maid to wait on me. So I did. Oh! 'tis a shame, 'tis a shame, 'tis a *shame.*'

Well, the Fairy was disappointed because she did hope she would have been pleased. But she said, 'Well, never you mind. When you go to bed tonight, just you turn round three times, and when you wake up in the morning you'll see what you'll see!'

So the Old Woman went to bed in the little white house with the pink curtains at the windows and the roses and honeysuckle – and the flowers and vegetables in the garden – and the pig in the sty. And she turned round three times. And when she woke up in the morning – someone was standing by her bed, saying, 'Please, ma'am, I've brought you a cup o' tea.' And when she opened her eyes and looked, there was a little maid to help her do her work; and she'd brought the Old

4

Woman a cup of tea to drink before she got out of bed. And when the Old Woman had drunk her tea, she got up and looked out of the window. And it *was* a little red brick house, and it *was* on the edge of the town, and she could see the folk going by to market!

Well, the Old Woman was pleased. But she never *thought* to say 'Thank you' to the Fairy.

Well, the Fairy she went East and she went West, and she went North and she went South; and one day she came back to where the Old Woman was living in the little red brick house, on the edge of the town, and where she could see the folks going by to market. And the Fairy said to herself, 'I'll just go and take a look at her. She *will* be pleased!'

But, do you know, when the Fairy stood on the Old Woman's door-step, she could hear (through the key-hole) the Old Woman talking to herself. (The Fairy wasn't *listening* at the key-hole. It was just as high as her ear, and she couldn't help hearing.) And *what* do you think she was saying? 'Oh! 'tis a shame,' said the Old Woman, ' 'tis a shame, so it is, 'tis a shame. Why should *I* live in a *little* house, when other folks live in *big* houses in

5

the middle of the town, with white steps up to the door, and men and maids to wait on them, and a carriage and pair to go driving in? Why shouldn't *I* live in a *big* house, in the middle of the town, with white steps up to the door, and men and maids to wait on me, and a carriage and pair to go driving in? 'Tis a shame, 'tis a shame, so it is, '*tis* a shame!'

Well, the Fairy was disappointed, because she did *hope* she would have been pleased. But she said, 'Well, never you mind. When you go to bed tonight, just you turn round three times, and when you wake up in the morning you'll see what you'll see!'

So the Old Woman went to bed that night in the little red brick house on the edge of town, where she could see folks going by to market. And she turned round three times, and when she woke up in the morning she was in the grandest bed she had ever seen! It had brass knobs at the top and brass knobs at the bottom; the Old Woman had never seen a bed like that before. And when she got up and looked out of the window, it *was* a big house, and it *was* in the middle of town, and there were white steps up to the door and men and maids to wait on her, and a carriage and pair to go driving in.

Well, the Old Woman was pleased. But she *never* thought to say 'Thank you' to the Fairy.

Well, the Fairy she went East and she went West, and she went North and she went South; and one day she came back to the town where the Old Woman was living in the big house, in the middle of the town, with white steps up to the door and men and maids to wait on her, and a carriage and pair to go driving in. And the Fairy said to herself, 'I'll just go and take a look at her. She *will* be pleased.'

But do you know, as soon as the Fairy stood inside the Old Woman's door, she could hear the Old Woman talking to herself, and *what* do you think she was saying? 'Oh! 'tis a shame,' said the Old Woman, ' 'tis a shame, so it is, 'tis a shame. *Look* at the Queen,' said the Old Woman, 'sitting on a gold throne, and living in a Palace, with a gold crown on her head, and red velvet carpet to walk on. Why shouldn't *I* be a Queen and sit on a gold throne and live in a Palace, with a gold crown on my head and red velvet carpet to walk on? 'Tis a shame, 'tis a shame, so it is, 'tis a *shame*.'

Well, the Fairy was disappointed because she *did* think she would have been pleased. But she said, 'Well-l-l-l, never you mind. When you go to bed tonight, just you turn round three times, and when you wake up in the morning you'll see what you'll see.'

So the Old Woman went to sleep in the grand bed with the brass knobs at the top and the brass knobs at the bottom, in the big house, in the middle of the town, with white steps up to the door, and men and maids to wait on her, and a carriage and pair to go driving in. And she turned round three times, and when she woke up in the morning she was in the grandest bed that ever was seen, with a red satin coverlet, and there was red velvet carpet by the side of the bed, and a gold crown on a table all ready to put on when she dressed. So the Old Woman got up and dressed and put on the gold crown, and walked on the red velvet carpet, and there was a gold throne to sit on. And the Old Woman was pleased. *But she never thought to say 'Thank you' to the Fairy.*

Well, the Fairy she went East and she went West, and she went North and she went South, and one day she came back to the town where the

Old Woman was living in the Palace, with a gold crown on her head and a gold throne to sit on and a red velvet carpet to walk on. And the Fairy said to herself, 'I'll just go and take a look at her. She *will* be pleased.'

So she walked right in at the Palace door, and up the red velvet stairs till she came to where the Old Woman was sitting on a gold throne with a gold crown on her head. And as soon as the Old Woman *saw* the Fairy she opened her mouth and *what* do you think she said? 'Oh! 'tis a shame,' said the Old Woman, ' 'tis a shame, so it is, 'tis a shame. This throne is most uncomfortable, the crown is too heavy for my head and there's a draught down the back of my neck. This is a most *inconvenient* house. Why *can't* I get a home to suit me? 'Tis a shame, 'tis a shame, so it is, '*tis* a shame.'

'Oh, very well,' said the Fairy. 'If all you want is just a house to suit you, when you go to bed tonight, just you turn round three times, and when you wake up in the morning you'll see what you'll see,' said the Fairy.

So the Old Woman went to bed that night in the Palace, in the big bed with the red satin coverlet and the red velvet carpet by the side of the bed, and the gold crown on the table all ready to put on in the morning. And she turned round three times (there was *plenty* of room to do it).

And when she woke up in the morning – she was BACK IN THE VINEGAR-BOTTLE. And she *stayed* there the rest of her life!

Papa Hedgehog and the Hare

It had been a very wet day. The rain had poured steadily from the grey sky; the birds had stayed quiet in the trees and hedges; and all the little creatures of the woods and fields had kept snug in their holes and burrows. But towards evening the rain had stopped, the sky cleared, and the sun shone out as if he was pleased to see all the world looking so bright and clean after the washing the clouds had given it.

Papa Hedgehog came creeping out of his hole (it was underneath a thick blackthorn bush, just on the edge of the wood). He looked round him. 'I think,' he said to his wife, ' I shall take a little walk in the cabbage field. It is a fine evening and so fresh after the rain. Really it is a pleasure to watch those cabbages grow, so large and handsome as they are and so cool and shady when the sun is hot. Besides,' said Papa Hedgehog, 'one finds delightful company there. The beetles are quite the pleasantest I have ever met.'

(I am afraid the beetles were more pleasant to Papa Hedgehog than he was to the beetles. For to tell the truth, he liked them so much that he *ate* them! But that has nothing to do with this story.)

'Do go, my love,' said Mamma Hedgehog. 'I will follow you as soon as possible. As you say, it is a fine evening, and a walk will do you good.'

So Papa Hedgehog trotted off on his four little legs, with his bright eyes and sharp nose, finding all kinds of good things to see and smell. The cabbages certainly were very handsome; their leaves were so broad and firm and green, and large, round, shining raindrops lay on them, sparkling like the clearest crystal. Papa Hedgehog sipped a little water from the hollow of a leaf and trotted on, keeping a sharp look-out for the beetles whose company he enjoyed so much.

Suddenly there was a scurry and a scuffle among the cabbages, and – almost on top of Papa Hedgehog – out bounced a large brown Hare, sending a shower of raindrops flying and upsetting quite a little pool of water from a big leaf over Papa Hedgehog's head and into his eyes and nose. Papa Hedgehog was startled, and he did as he always does when anything frightens him – he rolled himself into a tight little ball and stayed quite still for some minutes. Then he cautiously began to unroll, and the first thing his little bright eyes lit upon was the Hare sitting there laughing.

Papa Hedgehog sneezed and shook his head. He was a good-natured little fellow, and though the Hare had startled him he was not vexed. But if you or I had upset water all over a respectable old gentleman who was out for an evening walk we should at least say, 'I am sorry.' The Hare did nothing of the kind. He laughed and laughed till he nearly fell over with laughing. 'You can't think how funny you looked,' he said. 'You hedgehogs are funny anyhow, all just alike, with your round bodies and crooked legs. But I never saw you look so ridiculous as you did just now. Oh, dear! Oh, dear! Oh, dear!' said the Hare. And this time he

15

really did fall over sideways with laughing.

'My legs are very good and useful legs,' said Papa Hedgehog in a dignified voice, 'and they are much better than your *manners*, which are very bad indeed. Good evening,' said Papa Hedgehog, and he turned round to go home again, for the Hare had quite upset him and spoiled his evening walk. But the Hare shouted 'Crooked-legs' so loudly after him that he stopped. A thought came into his little head, and he smiled to himself. 'The Hare says we are all alike and all ridiculous, does he? Well, he shall see. It is time he had a lesson,' said Papa Hedgehog.

So he came trotting back. 'My legs may be crooked,' he said to the Hare, 'but that is no reason why you should laugh at them. Let us run a race and see who is the winner. You may be very much surprised!'

'A race indeed,' said the Hare; 'I can run a mile while you creep a yard.'

'Try and see,' said Papa Hedgehog. 'It is moonlight tonight, and the next field has been ploughed. I will run up one furrow. You shall run up the next. When you get to the end you shall see!'

'Very well, old Crooked-legs,' said the rude Hare; 'I'll be there, waiting to laugh at you.' And away he went with a hop, skip and jump of his long legs, over the bank, through the hedge, and across the fields, while Papa Hedgehog trotted home to his wife.

'My love,' said he, 'we are to play a little game with the Hare tonight,' and he told Mamma Hedgehog his plan; and they both chuckled so much that they rolled themselves into tight balls with laughing.

Presently – just a little while before the moon rose – Mamma Hedgehog trotted out and away into the dark. Papa Hedgehog had told her where to go and what to do, and by-and-by, when the moon was up, he followed. Past the cabbage field, where the cabbages looked as if they were made of ivory and silver in the moonlight, he scuttled – through the hedge – and there lay the ploughed field with its long, deep, dark furrows. A minute or two later the Hare came running swiftly along the edge of the field. 'Hullo, old Crooked-legs,' he said, 'are you ready to start?'

'Yes,' said Papa Hedgehog. 'I am quite ready. I will take the furrow nearest the hedge. You take the next. Are you ready? *Off!*'

Away went the Hare, bounding easily up the furrow. He did not hurry very much; he thought there was no need. 'Poor fellow,' he said scornfully to himself, 'his crooked legs must be working very hard to carry that fat little round body. Probably he will die for want of breath before he is half-way up the furrow. Well, it is not my fault,' said the Hare. And with one long jump he reached the end of the course. But just as he got there, a little head with two bright eyes and a sharp nose peeped out of the next furrow, and a little voice said, 'Here I am, you see!' It was Mamma Hedgehog who was waiting for him; but the Hare did not know that. One hedgehog looked just like another to him, especially by moonlight, and he thought Papa Hedgehog had got there first! His big eyes nearly popped out of his head with surprise. He did not wait one minute to think. 'I'll beat you next time,' he said in a great hurry; and he turned round and flew down the furrow, leaving Mamma Hedgehog chuckling behind him.

'Fancy old Crooked-legs running so fast,' said the Hare to himself as he ran, 'but he can never keep it up. He is probably dead by now!'

But when he was nearly at the end of the course a little head with a sharp nose and two bright eyes peeped out of the next furrow, and a little voice said, 'Here I am, you see!' It was Papa Hedgehog, who had been sitting there very comfortably, waiting for him.

'*You!*' said the Hare, very much out of breath. 'Yes, *me,*' said Papa Hedgehog. 'I'll beat you next time,' said the Hare, and he raced up the furrow again. But Mamma Hedgehog was ready for him, and back went the Hare once more. Up and down he raced, up and down. The time went by, and the

20

full moon came sailing higher and higher up the sky. It seemed as if there was a broad smile on its face at the sight of the Hare running so fast along the furrow, while Papa and Mamma Hedgehog waited for him, one at each end. Up and down he went, up and down; he was all out of breath, he was giddy and panting and puzzled. It was really a terrible race! And at last he was so tired he really could run no more; right in the middle of the furrow he tumbled down and went to sleep, and never woke up till sunrise next morning. And Papa and Mamma Hedgehog trotted off chuckling, to find their supper, and then they went home to sleep.

As for the Hare, next time he saw Papa Hedgehog coming, he went a long way round to avoid meeting him. He was afraid Papa Hedgehog would laugh! How the tale of the race came to be told I do not know; Papa and Mamma Hedgehog are quiet folk and do not talk much, and certainly the Hare never spoke of it. Perhaps it was the Man in the Moon! But whoever told it first, it has certainly been told a great many times since, and now I'm telling it again for you.

The Tale of the Talkative Tortoise

Mr and Mrs Duck were sitting in the nice cool grass at the edge of a pool, tidying their brown feathers (they were wild ducks and wild ducks are brown) with their yellow beaks and talking quietly and comfortably before they went to sleep.

It was a nice pool in a little valley among the hills. There was green grass round it, and little pink and white and yellow flowers grew in the grass, and there were slugs and snails to eat and fish in the pool. Mr and Mrs Duck had been most comfortable there. But they were not feeling very happy just now, because – there was no doubt about it – the pool was drying up. Every day there was a little more mud and a little less water, the rushes were beginning to look brown, and the grass looked thirsty. Soon there would not be enough water for Mr and Mrs Duck to swim in. 'We shall have to move away, I'm afraid,' said Mrs Duck with a sad little quack.

'Yes,' said Mr Duck, 'it looks like it. We shall have to fly over the hill and find another pool. That is easy to do. The thing that troubles me is the Tortoise. What will *he* do with no one to talk to?'

'Yes, that is quite true,' said Mrs Duck, with a tear in her little bright, black eye, for she was a kind-hearted creature; 'he will be terribly lonely.'

I had better explain about the Tortoise. He was only a very little tortoise who lived in the soft mud of the pool. Sometimes he buried himself and slept for weeks; perhaps it was because he had such long, long sleeps that he talked so much when he was awake, for he certainly was a terrible talker – and so proud! Just because he had a hard shell on his back, he despised the frogs with their soft skins, and was so rude to the fishes that if they put their heads out and saw him, they pulled them in again. As for the slugs and snails and beetles – he simply pretended they were not there.

So, for want of anyone better, he used to talk to himself for hours together – until Mr and Mrs Duck came to the pool. He found them most kind and amiable, and able to tell him of so many places and such wonderful things, that actually he began to listen sometimes instead of talking quite so much and despising everyone but himself.

Still, it was generally the Tortoise who talked, sitting in the mud at the edge of the pool on cool

25

evenings, while Mr and Mrs Duck swam about and said 'quack' softly every now and then. They were good listeners. 'And of course, my dear,' Mr Duck used to say, 'if the poor fellow talks *too* much we can just take a flight and exercise our wings a little for a change.' (Just as you or I would say, 'I am tired of being indoors; I will go for a walk.')

And away they would go for an hour or two, and the Tortoise was always very glad to see them come back.

But this was different. This meant going away for a long time – perhaps for always – and when they told the Tortoise about it he was terribly unhappy and actually cried; and if you look at a tortoise and see how dry and wrinkled he is, you can see what a lot it would take to make him *cry*.

'Can't I go with you?' he used to say every evening after that when they talked of going. The pool was getting terribly small; they would certainly have to go soon; but it seemed absurd to think of his going with them. It worried their kind hearts. Till suddenly, one day Mr Duck said to Mrs Duck, 'I believe we could do it!'

'What is it, dear?' said Mrs Duck, looking at him

affectionately, with her little black eye. (Ducks are *very* affectionate.)

'I believe we could *carry* him,' said Mr Duck. 'He has strong teeth and a remarkably tough neck, almost like leather, and if he held on to a piece of stick with his teeth, you and I could each take an end of it, and we could carry him between us!'

'If only he *did* hold on,' said Mrs Duck. 'You know how fond he is of talking, and I don't believe he could ever keep his mouth shut.' And you will see – just as plainly as Mrs Duck did – that it is quite impossible to hold on to a stick with your teeth and open your mouth to talk at the same time.

'Well,' said Mr Duck, 'I will talk to him, and we can but try.'

So they explained their plan to the Tortoise, and he was delighted. And all that evening, as Mr and Mrs Duck swam about on the pool (it was hardly more than a puddle by this time), the Tortoise sat in the mud and talked of the wonderful journey, and told them how quiet he could be if he tried.

Very early next morning Mr Duck went to look for a nice piece of stick, and presently he came back with one just the right thickness and just the right length. The Tortoise took hold in the middle, the Ducks took hold of each end. 'Ready?' said Mr Duck. 'Keep your mouth *shut*,' said Mrs Duck. The Tortoise winked both eyes hard to show that he heard. Mr and Mrs Duck spread their strong wings and away they went. Higher and higher they rose, the little pool shone in the sunlight far below them and over the hills and far away flew Mr and Mrs Duck with friend Tortoise hanging between them.

'Quack?' Mr Duck would say now and again. (Ducks can quack without opening their bills.) 'Quack, quack,' Mrs Duck would say, and the Tortoise would wink his eyes to show he heard them and was quite safe and comfortable. It all sounds so pleasant that I am really sorry to have to tell you the end of the story.

By and by they came in sight of a village. 'A little higher, my dear,' said Mr Duck; 'there might be boys with stones there,' and 'Quack, quack,' said Mrs Duck. At the sound of their voices a little boy looked up and called to another boy. 'Oh! Look! *Look!* The ducks are carrying a tortoise!'; and the other boy said, 'Oh, look, look, look!' and his sister heard him, and she called, 'Oh, look, look, look!'

and their mother heard them, and she called to her next-door neighbour, 'Oh, look, look, look, look!' till the village was full of people all pointing and laughing and saying, 'Look, look, look!'

It hurt friend Tortoise's feelings terribly. He blinked his eyes and nearly choked with rage.

'Quack,' said Mrs Duck soothingly. 'Quack, quack,' said Mr Duck sharply, which meant 'Keep quiet'; but it was too late. 'Silly creatures,' shrieked the Tortoise, and I don't know how much more he meant to say, but oh dear! Oh dear! He had opened his mouth and let go of the stick!

Mr and Mrs Duck flapped steadily on, but the Tortoise was gone – down and down he fell till he landed in somebody's garden, and there he had to stay, with no one but frogs and toads and slugs and snails and beetles to talk to for the rest of his life, and very dull he found it. His kind friends, Mr and Mrs Duck, could never come back to fetch him; there were too many people in the village who would have liked roast duck for dinner.

I am sorry for the Tortoise. His sad story has been handed down to all the members of the Tortoise family, as a warning not to talk too much;

and if you have ever met a tortoise you will know that he is a very quiet creature now, and seldom, if ever, makes a sound.

The Tale of Mrs Puffin's Prize Pumpkin

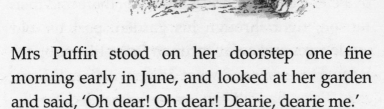

Mrs Puffin stood on her doorstep one fine morning early in June, and looked at her garden and said, 'Oh dear! Oh dear! Dearie, dearie me.'

You could not really say there was much garden to look at. There had been no rain for weeks and everything was dried up. The rose that climbed over the house was covering the ground with white petals like snow; the honeysuckle was drooping, and the tall foxgloves by the door hung their heads. Even the pinks in the border looked shrivelled, and Mrs Puffin's neat rows of young cabbages and potatoes and peas were thirsty and dry.

'I'll go down the hill,' said Mrs Puffin, 'and get a bucket or two of water and give the peas a soaking before the sun gets hot.'

Mrs Puffin lived in a little white cottage half-way up a hill. If you went down a lane between tall green hedges you came to another little white house at the bottom of the hill where her nearest neighbour lived. His name was Peter Pinch. Peter had a garden too, but in spite of the hot dry weather it was still fresh and green. A tiny spring of clear, bright water came out of the hillside just by Peter's gate. It made a little pool there and then ran on, right through his garden, past his old apple-trees and away through fields till I suppose it came to a river and went down with it to the sea.

So Peter had all the water he needed for his garden. His roses were pink and white and covered with buds; his flowers stood up straight and strong, his cabbages and potatoes and peas looked fresh and green. You would not think Peter had anything to grumble about. But he had. He grumbled every day and every time when Mrs Puffin came to fetch water from his little pool.

'Don't take too much, Mrs Puffin,' he would say, 'you'll empty the pool and leave none for me.

Two buckets full in the morning and two in the evening is a-plenty,' said Peter.

He knew quite well that the little spring went on running, and that however much water Mrs Puffin took, the pool would soon fill again. But Peter Pinch always wanted to keep everything for himself. Even the birds made him angry. He threw stones at them to drive them away from his garden in summer, and he never gave them even a crumb in winter.

On the morning that I am telling you about, Mrs Puffin hoped that Peter Pinch would still be asleep. She went quietly down the hill with her buckets. It was not really very far, though it seemed a long way when you came uphill with a heavy bucket in each hand. She looked up at Peter's window and saw that it was shut and the curtains were drawn. So she did not hurry. She dipped the water out of the little pool, slowly and comfortably with her big tin mug, till the pails were nearly full. Then she carried them up and watered her thirsty peas and went down again to get water for the house.

She had filled one bucket and was stooping over the second when somebody laughed and something fell with a loud splash into her pail.

Mrs Puffin jumped, and said, 'Bless me!' and looked round. Peter Pinch was leaning over his gate, laughing to himself. He had just dropped a large toad into the full bucket. Toads do not like being dropped into water any more than you or I would, so Mrs Puffin said, 'Poor thing!' and picked him out in a hurry and wrapped him in two dock-leaves and put him in her apron pocket. She was sure Peter did not mean to be kind to the toad, so she would not leave him there.

Peter only laughed again and said, 'There's a bit of company for you, Mrs Puffin. I've got no room for him in *my* garden.'

And Mrs Puffin said politely in a dignified voice, 'Good *morning*, Mr Pinch,' and picked up her pails and went up the hill. She put the toad down in a cool corner under some ferns by the door; and she used the water from the pail he had been in for scrubbing. There was enough in the other pail to make several cups of tea, so she did not have to go down the hill again till the cool of the day was come.

When she came back with her pails in the evening, she found the toad sitting on her doorstep. He looked at her with his bright eyes,

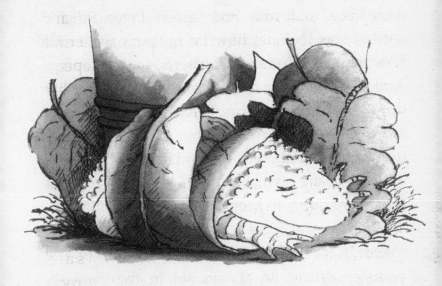

and Mrs Puffin nodded at him, 'Good evening, Master Toad,' she said, 'I hope I see you well.'

When she had finished watering her garden he was still there, and she said good night to him when she shut the door. He was among her rows of peas next morning when she watered them, and Mrs Puffin said, 'Nice morning' to him. The toad never made a sound – as you know, toads are quiet creatures – but he looked fat and comfortable, and as the days went by Mrs Puffin talked to him more and more. When she came panting up the hill with her buckets, she used to tell him how hot it was and how heavy the pails were. She told him how green Peter Pinch's garden was looking, how fat his peas were and how rosy and ripe his strawberries were getting. And at last, one evening, poor Mrs Puffin sat down and burst into tears. Peter Pinch had been so cross, she was so tired, and her garden looked so dried up and withered. 'If only I had a little spring of water of my own,' said poor Mrs Puffin, 'just a little tiny spring, to keep the garden green!'

She cried and cried and the toad looked at her solemnly. He was sitting in the corner of the doorstep where he always sat in the evening. Presently he crawled off the doorstep and went slowly down the garden path. He wriggled under Mrs Puffin's gate; she thought he must be going down the lane, but she was too tired and miserable to go and look. She cried a little more, because she was really fond of her toad and she was afraid he was tired of her dried-up garden, and then she went to bed.

But when she came out with her pails very early next morning, she saw the toad again. He had not gone down the hill, after all. He was crawling under the gate of a field, a little way down the lane.

'Good morning, Master Toad,' said Mrs Puffin. The toad sat in the lane and looked wisely at her, and Mrs Puffin looked over the gate. The grass in the field was short because Farmer Brown's cows fed there, and she could see very plainly that there was a big fairy-ring in the middle of the field. And from the fairy-ring to the gate there was a little ruffled pathway through the dew, as if something had crawled across the grass.

'It seems to *me*,' said Mrs Puffin to herself as she went down the hill, 'that my Master Toad has been talking to the Fairies!'

When she came back the toad was in the garden again, and in the evening he was on the doorstep as usual, so Mrs Puffin knew he had come back to stay.

It was not long after this that a fat, juicy green shoot came up in the corner of Mrs Puffin's garden, in a little hollow by the hedge. Mrs Puffin looked at it and wondered what it could be, and gave it all the water she could spare to encourage it to grow.

It grew very fast and presently Mrs Puffin said, 'It's a pumpkin plant. Wherever did it come from?' She looked at the toad as if he could tell her. She thought perhaps he could, if only he could talk. She had not forgotten the morning when she saw him coming away from the fairy-ring. 'And maybe,' she said to herself, 'the Good Folks sent me a pumpkin plant to make up for the rest of my things being spoiled this year!'

Pumpkins are rather like vegetable marrows. They like plenty of water. Mrs Puffin gave her pumpkin every drop she could spare. She emptied her scrubbing-pail and her washing-bowl into the hollow. She put all her tea-leaves round the root to keep it damp. And the pumpkin grew big green leaves and long green stalks and it blossomed with large yellow flowers.

Mrs Puffin watched it grow with joy and pride. She was so proud of it that she even told Peter Pinch about it, and he used to walk up the lane to look at it and count the flowers and wonder how many pumpkins there would be. He had none of his own, and to tell the truth he was rather jealous of Mrs Puffin. So I am afraid he was really pleased to find that when all the yellow flowers had fallen, there was only one little green pumpkin left.

Mrs Puffin was very disappointed. She had hoped she was going to have half a dozen pumpkins at least. But she only said, 'One is a deal better than none,' and she went on watering her pumpkin plant. And the little pumpkin grew and grew and *grew*, larger and larger, rounder and rounder till it was a most enormous pumpkin! Mrs Puffin watched it grow. She went to look at it so often that her footsteps made quite a deep little pathway across her garden. Very often she found the toad sitting in the little hollow, and she thought to herself, 'He's as proud of it as I am.'

When September came the pumpkin was ripe. It had turned from green to pale yellow and from

yellow to bright orange. The leaves and stalks dried up and withered, but the pumpkin almost filled the little hollow. It lay there like a large round golden moon. And it was heavy. Mrs Puffin moved it gently and felt sure she could not lift it. She said to Peter Pinch, 'My pumpkin's ripe, Master Pinch. I shall cut it this evening for fear it should spoil. If you like to come up the hill, I'll give you half of it. There's more than I can use.'

Peter Pinch was pleased. He liked having presents given to him, though he never gave any himself. So about six o'clock that evening he went up the hill and found Mrs Puffin with a knife, all ready to cut the pumpkin.

'I'll cut it in half in the garden,' said Mrs Puffin, 'it's too heavy to carry into the house.'

She stooped down to cut it. But as the point of her knife went into the big yellow pumpkin, Mrs Puffin said, '*Oh!*' in a startled voice. 'Oh!' she said. 'Oh dear! It's quite hollow. There's nothing in it, Master Pinch!'

She pulled out the knife and there was a little bubbling sound. A tiny stream of water ran out of the hole that the knife had made.

Peter Pinch looked at it angrily. 'That pumpkin's

bad,' he said. And he turned round and stomped away down the hill, very cross indeed. He was really a very grumpy old man.

Poor Mrs Puffin! She was dreadfully disappointed. She went in and sat down and made herself a large cup of tea for comfort; and she did not go out into the garden again that evening. She could not bear to look at her beautiful pumpkin.

But she looked out of her window that night before she got into bed. She remembered she had not said good night to the toad. It was a clear night with a great bright moon, and she could see Master Toad quite plainly sitting by the little hollow. The pumpkin lay there, but she could see only part of it. The hollow was almost filled with clear water that shone in the moonlight and the pumpkin was nearly covered.

'It must have held a lot of water. It's a very odd pumpkin,' said Mrs Puffin. Then she called 'Good night' to the toad and she got into bed and went to sleep.

When she came out early next morning with her pails, the first thing she noticed was a little stream – a tiny sparkling stream of water, running from the pumpkin hollow, along the little path that her footsteps had made right across her garden.

'Bless me!' said Mrs Puffin, 'where did that come from? That pumpkin gets odder and odder.'

She hurried across her garden to see what could have happened. When she came to the hollow, Master Toad sat by it looking at it solemnly and importantly. Mrs Puffin looked too; she was looking for her big pumpkin. But there was no pumpkin to be seen. The little hollow was filled with clear water that stirred and rippled gently as if it bubbled up softly from beneath.

'Oh-h-h-h!' said Mrs Puffin – and she said no more for quite a long while – as she stood there looking and thinking.

Presently she stooped down and looked close; under the ripples she thought she could just see a gleam of yellow shining. 'Yes,' said Mrs Puffin, and she nodded her head. 'Yes, that's it, there's my pumpkin. It was a fairy pumpkin, sure enough. The Good Folks sent it to me with a spring of water in it for my garden!'

She turned and curtseyed very deeply and gratefully to the toad and said, 'Thank you, Master Toad, my dear.' She was sure he was pleased because his eyes sparkled like little diamonds in the sunlight.

Then Mrs Puffin put her pails on the doorstep and hurried down the hill. She stopped to make a curtsey and to say 'Thank you with all my heart,' in the middle of the fairy-ring; and then she ran to Peter Pinch's cottage. She knocked on the door and threw little stones at the window till Peter Pinch opened it and put out his head (with a night-cap on it), very cross indeed at being waked so early.

Mrs Puffin said, 'Peter Pinch! I've got a spring of water in my garden. It's come from my big pumpkin,' which surprised him so much that he came running downstairs in two minutes, all dressed, with his night-cap still on his head.

They went up the hill together; and there was no doubt about it, there really was a spring. The water bubbled up softly in the pool in the hollow and flowed through Mrs Puffin's garden and into the field and down the hill.

'I shall never have to carry pails of water up the hill again,' said Mrs Puffin. And she never did. Spring, summer, autumn, and winter, the water flowed and Mrs Puffin's garden was green and blossoming every year.

She and Master Toad lived there in great happiness and contentment for many years after. And I am glad to say that even Peter Pinch grew bettertempered when Mrs Puffin no longer needed to draw water from his spring. On summer evenings he would often hobble up the hill for a chat; and they would talk together of Mrs Puffin's prize pumpkin, while Master Toad sat by them on the doorstep.

Father Sparrow's Tug-of-war

Father Sparrow was perched on a twig, talking very fast and very loud to Mother Sparrow, who was sitting on a nest full of eggs. It was early in the day; the sun was shining brightly, the monkeys were chattering, birds were hopping and chirping – it was a pleasant morning, but Father Sparrow was cross.

He had been down to the river to bathe, in a nice shallow place he knew of, and there was the Crocodile, half in and half out of the water, filling up the whole of the bathing-place! And when Father Sparrow scolded him, he only opened his mouth wide and laughed (it was a *very* wide mouth), and said, lazily, 'I shall stay here just as long as I please.'

So Father Sparrow was very cross, and as I have said, he was telling Mother Sparrow all about it, when suddenly, *bump*, somebody very big crashed against the tree, which rocked and swayed so that Father Sparrow nearly fell off his twig; and if Mother Sparrow had not sat very tight the eggs would certainly have rolled out of the nest.

'Really there is no peace in the forest this morning,' said Father Sparrow still more crossly (and I think he had some excuse). 'Now, who can that be?'

He flew down to see, and there was a big grey back and a little grey tail disappearing amongst the trees. It was Brother Elephant taking a walk in the forest.

'Stop, Brother Elephant!' said Father Sparrow with a loud chirp. 'Do you know that you have nearly shaken my wife off her nest?'

'Well,' said Brother Elephant, 'I don't mind if I have.' Which, of course, was very rude of him; he might at least have said he was sorry.

'You don't mind!' twittered Father Sparrow.

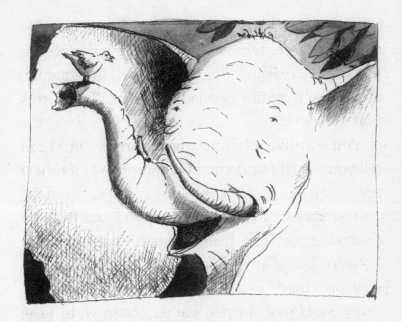

'You don't mind! I'll make you mind, Brother Elephant, and if you shake my nest again, *I'll tie you up!*'

Mother Sparrow gave a little chirp of surprise and Brother Elephant chuckled. 'Tie me up then,' he said, 'you're quite welcome to do it; but you can't keep me tied, Father Sparrow, not even if a thousand sparrows tried!'

'*Wait and see,*' said Father Sparrow. Brother Elephant trumpeted with laughter and went crashing and trampling through the forest, and after a little talk with Mother Sparrow, Father

Sparrow flew down to the river. The Crocodile was still there, fast asleep and filling up all the bathing-place. Father Sparrow chirped indignantly, and the Crocodile opened one eye. 'I like this place,' he said.

'You may like it,' said Father Sparrow, 'but I can tell you this, if I find you here tomorrow *I'll tie you up!*'

'You may tie me as much as you like,' said the Crocodile, shutting his eye again, 'but you can't keep me tied, Father Sparrow – not if a thousand sparrows tried.'

'*Wait and see,*' chirped Father Sparrow; but the Crocodile was fast asleep again. So Father Sparrow flew away.

He was very busy all that morning, talking to all his sparrow friends, and next day they were all up very early and working hard. There were quite a thousand of them, and they had a long, long piece of a creeper that grows in the forest, and is nearly as strong as the strongest rope.

Presently Brother Elephant came crashing through the forest. *Bump!* he went against Father Sparrow's tree. (Mother Sparrow was expecting him, so she was not shaken much.) 'Well,' said

Brother Elephant, 'here I am! Are you going to tie me up, Father Sparrow?'

'Yes,' chirped Father Sparrow, ' I am going to tie you up and hold you tight.' And he and all the other sparrows pulled, and pecked, and hopped and tugged, and fluttered (you can imagine the noise they made), till the rope – it was really a creeper, of course, but we will call it a rope – was tight around Brother Elephant's big body.

'Now Brother Elephant,' said Father Sparrow, 'when I say "Pull", *pull*.'

'So I will,' said Brother Elephant, shaking with laughter; and he waited, while Father Sparrow and all the other sparrows flew away with the rope, tugging it through bushes and tall reeds to the riverside. There was the Crocodile, in Father Sparrow's bathing-place, and when he saw them he laughed.

'Have you and your friends come to tie me up, Father Sparrow?' he said.

'Yes,' said Father Sparrow. 'I am going to tie you up and hold you tight.'

'Tie away,' said the Crocodile; and the sparrows pulled, and pecked, and chattered, and tugged, and hopped, till the rope was tight round the

Crocodile's long body.

'Now,' said Father Sparrow, 'when I say "Pull",
pull.'

The Crocodile was too lazy too answer; he only
chuckled till the water rippled round him, and the
sparrows flew away.

Then Father Sparrow perched himself on the
middle of the rope among the bushes, where
neither Brother Elephant nor the Crocodile could
see him; and of course neither of them could see
the other. *'Pull,'* cried Father Sparrow in a very
loud chirp, and Brother Elephant gave a great tug.

'That will surprise Father Sparrow,' he said. But

it was really Brother Elephant who was surprised, because from the other end of the line came such a jerk that he was nearly pulled off his feet. Of course he thought it was Father Sparrow but, as you know, it was the Crocodile, who never meant to trouble to pull at all; he was far too lazy! *He* thought it was Father Sparrow pulling too, and was even more surprised than Brother Elephant.

'What a strong sparrow he is!' said the Crocodile.

'How hard Father Sparrow can pull,' said Brother Elephant, and they both pulled and pulled and pulled and *pulled*.

Sometimes Brother Elephant pulled hardest and the Crocodile was nearly pulled out of the river. Sometimes the Crocodile gave a jerk, and Brother Elephant had to twist his trunk round a tree and hold on. They were really just about equal, and neither could move the other an inch. It was a wonderful tug-of-war. The sun rose high in the sky and began to creep down towards the west; they grew hot and thirsty and tired. The sparrows laughed at them when they puffed and grunted and panted. Each of them thought, 'I wish I had not laughed at Father Sparrow.' And still they pulled and pulled and pulled – they were so very ashamed and tired.

At last, just as the sun was beginning to slip out of sight, Brother Elephant said in a very small voice: 'Please tell Father Sparrow that if he will stop pulling and untie me, I will never be rude to him again.'

Just at the same moment the Crocodile said to himself, 'All the animals will be coming to drink, and how they will laugh when they see me tied up here!' and he called, 'Please, Father Sparrow, stop pulling and untie me, and I will never take your bathing-place again.'

'Very well,' chirped Father Sparrow very loud; 'very well, very well' (which is the same as 'Hip, hip, hurrah!' would be for you and me), and the sparrows hopped, and pecked, and pulled, and chattered till they untied Brother Elephant, and he went away with his head hanging down, terribly ashamed of being beaten by Father Sparrow. They untied the Crocodile too, and he crawled in among the high reeds that grew by the river and hid himself, dreadfully cross because he had been tied up all day.

Neither of them ever knew they had really been pulling each other, and after this Brother Elephant walked quietly, so quietly, in the forest, and the Crocodile let Father Sparrow bathe in peace.

As for Father Sparrow, he and all his friends flew away and told their wives all about the tug-of-war. Then they put their little heads under their wings and all went fast asleep. It had been a very busy day!

The Tale of Mr and Mrs Peppercorn and Their Cuckoo-clock

Just in case you have never seen a cuckoo-clock I had better explain what it is before the story begins.

A cuckoo-clock is shaped like a little house made out of wood, with a pointed roof. Just under the point of the roof there is a tiny door. Under the door is a clock-face. Some clocks have a little bell that strikes 'ting-ting' to tell the hour; but a cuckoo-clock has a cuckoo. He is carved in wood and he lives just inside the tiny door. Every hour when the long hand of the clock reaches twelve the door clicks open and out pops the cuckoo.

'Cuckoo!' he says, and you count the cuckoo calls and you know what time it is.

And now I will tell you the story of Mr and Mrs Peppercorn and their cuckoo-clock.

Mr and Mrs Peppercorn lived in a little farm high up on a green hillside. Mrs Peppercorn was large and stout; Mr Peppercorn was small and thin. They had a little white house and a cat and a dog. They had two brown cows and a pig and a little grey donkey. They had a cock and some speckly hens and four ducks on a tiny pond. They were as busy and as happy as the day was long. Only sometimes in spring Mrs Peppercorn said to herself, 'I should like to be down in the woods to hear the cuckoo calling this fine sunshiny day, like I did when I was a little girl.' But she was too busy to go down, and she was very happy with Mr Peppercorn, so she did not think about the cuckoo very often.

It was a fine sunshiny day in June when this story happened. It was early in the morning and Mr Peppercorn had on his best clothes because he was going down the hillside with the little grey donkey to the town in the valley. He was taking butter and cheese and two big baskets of eggs to sell, and he was going to bring back tea and sugar and currants and flour and other things that Mrs Peppercorn needed. And besides all these he was going to bring back a present for Mrs Peppercorn. She did not know it, but he had been saving for that present for a very long time, and now he had five silver shillings in his pocket. He did not quite know what he was going to buy, but he felt sure it would be something very nice. So he went whistling down the hillside, and Mrs Peppercorn called after him, 'Don't you hurry back, my dear; take a bit of a holiday and enjoy yourself. And be sure you listen and tell me if you hear a cuckoo calling!'

Mr Peppercorn and the donkey went happily down the green hillside and through the green woods till they came to the town. They got there just as the shops were opening, and Mr Peppercorn soon sold all his eggs and butter and cheese. Then he bought the things that Mrs Peppercorn needed, and then he began to think about buying her present. But he could not make up his mind what he should buy. He thought of a new dress. 'But it might be the wrong size,' he said. He thought of a new hat. 'But it might be the wrong colour.' He thought of a silver brooch. 'But she has one already and she won't want another.' He thought of all kinds of things, but none of them seemed quite right.

He was beginning to feel very puzzled and muddled when he heard a great shouting and he saw a large fat man running after a small thin dog. The small thin dog had a very large bone and the large fat man had a very big stick. The dog was so frightened that it did not see where it was going. It ran straight up the road, and suddenly it turned and before Mr Peppercorn knew what was happening it ran between his feet. And down on his nose fell Mr Peppercorn, all mixed up with the dog and the bone, and the big man rushed up and stood over them with the big thick stick.

Everyone was laughing except the large fat man. He looked so cross that Mr Peppercorn felt sorry for the dog. He sat up and said, 'Please don't beat him.'

And the man said, 'I *will* beat him. He's stolen the bone that my wife was going to make soup with. I'll beat him well and tie him up. He won't have a chance to steal any more.'

Mr Peppercorn felt still more sorry for the dog.

He forgot all about Mrs Peppercorn's present. He only remembered that he had five silver shillings in his pocket and said, 'Don't do that. I'll buy the dog. I'll give you five shillings for him.'

The fat man said in a great hurry, 'You can have him,' and Mr Peppercorn, who was still sitting on the ground, felt in his pocket and gave him his five precious silver shillings.

The fat man went away very pleased, and Mr Peppercorn got up rather slowly and looked at the donkey. The donkey was looking rather surprised, and to tell the truth, Mr Peppercorn was surprised too. He knew he did not want another dog, and he did not suppose Mrs Peppercorn would want one either, and he was quite sure that Sammy, their old black dog, would not be at all pleased to see the little dog if he took it home. He did not know what to do.

He took the donkey to a stable and left him there munching hay, and then he walked a little way out of town and sat down under a tree to eat his dinner and think. His dinner was tied up in a large handkerchief. It was bread and bacon and cheese, with some radishes to munch. The small thin dog shared it with him, and it seemed so hungry that

Mr Peppercorn did not have much besides radishes for his dinner that day. He gave all the rest to the dog. When it was all eaten, they walked on a little farther.

Mr Peppercorn was still thinking what to do when they came to a cottage with a garden full of flowers. Mr Peppercorn knocked at the door. He wanted a drink of water for himself and some for the little dog.

An old woman came to the door, and when Mr Peppercorn said, 'Could I have some water for myself and the dog, if you please?' she said, 'Come in and sit down. I'll get you some and welcome.'

Mr Peppercorn sat down, and when the water came the dog lapped up a saucerful very quickly and curled himself up on the mat by the hearth as if he had lived there all his life. Mr Peppercorn drank his water slowly, and while he drank he told the old woman about his adventure with the large fat man and how he had spent all his money on the small thin dog. 'And now I don't know what to do with him,' he said.

The old woman sat listening, and when he had finished she sat there thinking and presently she nodded her head.

'He's a nice little dog,' she said, 'and if he was well fed he wouldn't steal. Give him to me; he'll be company for me, and I'll give you a pair of white rabbits for your wife.'

Mr Peppercorn thought that was a splendid idea. They went into the back garden; there were rows of carrots and lettuces and onions and potatoes and cabbages, and there was a big hutch with a whole family of fluffy white rabbits. Mr Peppercorn chose two. The old woman put them in a basket with some hay and a carrot to nibble. She tied down the lid, and Mr Peppercorn thanked her and took the basket. He went away down the road, happy and contented with his present for Mrs Peppercorn, and the old woman and the little dog looked happy and contented too. It all seemed as nice as could be.

There was plenty of time so he did not hurry; he sat down to rest under a tree. Presently a small boy came by with a long wooden cage in his hand, and as he came nearer Mr Peppercorn could see that there was a squirrel in the cage – a little brown squirrel from the woods. The boy looked happy but the squirrel did not. It sat in the cage all bunched up and miserable, and Mr Peppercorn said to himself, 'Oh dear! Oh dear! A squirrel in a cage!' And he said to the small boy, 'What are you going to do with the squirrel?'

The small boy said, 'Keep him in the cage for a pet.'

And Mr Peppercorn forgot all about Mrs Peppercorn's present. He only thought about a squirrel shut up in a cage when it ought to be racing up and down the trees in the wood among green leaves and swinging, swaying branches.

He said, 'Wouldn't you like two beautiful rabbits instead? Give the squirrel to me and you can have them.' And he opened the basket a little and let the small boy peep in.

The small boy looked and he said, 'O-oo-oh! *White* rabbits! You can have the squirrel!'

Mr Peppercorn gave him the basket and took the cage. The boy trotted off very happy and contented, and left Mr Peppercorn standing under the tree, considering. You know, of course, what he meant to do. He was going to let the squirrel go, as quickly as possible. He was only thinking where he could take it, and presently he trudged up the road again and turned into a little lane that ran between green hedges till it came to the edge of a wood. Mr Peppercorn stepped in among the trees and put the cage on the ground under a great beech-tree. Then he opened the door and stood back a little and watched.

The squirrel had been so frightened that it sat quite still for a minute and did not even seem to see the open door. Then suddenly it seemed to wake and it was out, running like a little red-brown streak across the rustling brown beech leaves and over mossy green roots to the big smooth grey trunk of the tree. Up the tree it went so nimbly, so lightly, so happily, with its tail fluffed out like a feather and its bright eyes shining. It stopped for a second where a big branch joined the trunk and looked down at Mr Peppercorn as if it was saying, 'Thank you and good-bye!' Then it went on, higher and higher, up and up, among the clear green leaves and the silver-grey branches till it was out of sight.

Mr Peppercorn stood watching till the squirrel had gone. Then he stooped and picked up the cage; and suddenly he remembered that he had no present for Mrs Peppercorn. There he was with no money in his pocket and an empty squirrel cage in his hand. He did not want the cage, and he did not want anyone else to have it, in case they should put another squirrel in it. He could not see what to do with it.

He was walking down the lane thinking what to do, when he heard the creaking of wheels. Round the corner came a yellow caravan drawn by an old white horse. On the step of the caravan sat an old man with a rosy face and a grey beard. He looked a nice old man, but when he saw Mr Peppercorn with the squirrel cage his face grew very cross.

'What are you doing with that squirrel cage?' he called grumpily. 'Nobody has any business to put a squirrel in a cage – no they haven't,' said the old man.

'I was just wondering what to do with it,' said Mr Peppercorn; and he told the old man about the squirrel and how he had set it free.

The old man smiled all over his face. His eyes twinkled and he grew rosier than ever with pleasure.

'I'll tell you what we'll do,' he said. 'I was just wanting a nice bit of dry wood to light my fire. All the sticks in the wood are damp after last night's rain. We'll make a fire with that cage and have a cup of tea.'

Mr Peppercorn was delighted. The old man got down from the caravan. They broke up the cage and lit a fire, and while the kettle boiled Mr Peppercorn told the old man all about his day's marketing and how hard he had tried to buy a present for Mrs Peppercorn. 'And here I am,' he said, rather sadly, 'with nothing to take back to her, after all.'

'Well,' said the old man, 'that was a nice cup of tea, wasn't it? – (Mr Peppercorn said, 'Thank you.') – I am very much obliged to you for giving me such a nice bit of dry wood to make my fire with. And now,' he said, 'I am going to give you a present to take back to your wife. I am going to give you a clock. My grandmother had three clocks and I have them all. Three clocks are too many for one caravan. Come inside and see.'

Mr Peppercorn went up the steps and in at the door and into the caravan. I wish I had time to tell you how nice it was, with its gay little window curtains and its shining paint and bright saucepans and china. But I can only tell you about the clocks. There were three of them, as the old man had said. One had a face like a moon – round and white with black numbers on it. One was large and long, in a wooden case with a coloured picture painted above the clock face and a solemn tick-tock-tick. The third clock sat on a little shelf in a corner and was quite quiet because it was not wound up. It looked like a little wooden house – a dear little brown house with a painted roof with wide edges carved into a pattern. Just under the roof was a little door like the doors you sometimes see in barns and stables. Below the little door was a clock face with white carved numbers and white carved hands.

Mr Peppercorn looked at the third clock and he thought it was lovely, and when the old man said, 'That's the clock for you,' his heart beat quite fast with happiness.

'That's the clock,' said the old man, and he took down the clock and unscrewed the little shelf and wrapped them up in a clean piece of potato sack and gave them to Mr Peppercorn.

'Here's the key,' he said, and his eyes twinkled. 'You'll get a surprise when you've wound that clock.'

Mr Peppercorn thanked him again and again, and trudged away down the road. His heart was filled with joy because he really had a present for Mrs Peppercorn. He turned several times to wave to the yellow caravan, and then he hurried down the hill and back to the town to get the donkey and the parcels. He packed his baskets carefully and put the clock in one of them, and then he and the donkey set out for home. Up through the woods they went and over the green hillside till they came to the little farm.

Mrs Peppercorn was standing at the gate watching for them. 'Well, my dear,' she said to Mr Peppercorn, 'did you have a nice day and did you hear a cuckoo calling?'

'No,' said Mr Peppercorn. 'I didn't hear a cuckoo calling, but I had a wonderful day and I've brought you a present, my dear.'

He unwrapped the clock and showed it her, and Mrs Peppercorn was as surprised and as pleased as could be. They put the donkey in the field to get his supper; and while Mrs Peppercorn bustled about the kitchen, Mr Peppercorn got his tools and he fixed up the little shelf for the clock. While he worked he told Mrs Peppercorn about his adventures, and she could hardly set the table for listening.

Then he wound the clock and put it in its place. It was just above the kitchen table, and as they sat at supper they could watch the white carved hand creeping from minute to minute and from one white number to another, while the short hand moved slowly until it was almost at six o'clock.

Suddenly Mr Peppercorn thought of something. 'The old man said there would be a surprise,' he said. 'I wonder what it can be?' And just as he said it, the surprise came. You have guessed, of course, but Mr and Mrs Peppercorn had not – and it certainly was a surprise!

The long hand of the clock touched twelve and the short hand touched six. There was a click as the little door above the clock face flew open and there stood a tiny bird beautifully carved in wood. It bobbed its head and flapped its wings and opened its little bill. 'Cuckoo,' said the little bird clearly and sweetly, 'cuckoo, cuckoo, cuckoo, cuckoo, cuckoo!' Then the little door shut with a snap and the bird was gone.

Mr and Mrs Peppercorn sat staring at the clock, too surprised to move or speak. They could hardly believe it was real. Mrs Peppercorn pinched herself and poked Mr Peppercorn to make certain that it was not a dream. 'If it happens again at seven o'clock, I shall know it's true,' she said.

And, of course, as you know, it did. The cuckoo popped out at seven o'clock and again at eight. They heard it faintly in the night and when they came down in the morning it was all ready to call 'Cuckoo!' seven times when they sat down to their breakfast at seven o'clock.

They soon got used to it and they always loved it. They even left the kitchen door open at night so that they could hear the cuckoo calling in the dark. 'It's easy to get up, even on a winter's morning, with that to call you,' said Mrs Peppercorn and she was not sorry any more that she could not go down the hill to hear the cuckoo in the woods in spring.

'Now we have a cuckoo-clock,' she often said cheerfully to Mr Peppercorn, 'it's spring-time in the house all year round.'

And Mr Peppercorn smiled happily at her and thought how lucky he was to have Mrs Peppercorn – and a cuckoo-clock into the bargain!

The Tale of Mr T Toad and Mr Littlefrog

There was once a pleasant little pool that lay in the corner of a large green field. Tall reeds and rushes grew round it in a ring, and beyond them were thorn bushes and brambles. So the little pool was hidden away from everyone but the birds who flew over it and the dragonflies that sometimes floated above it.

Down among the reeds and rushes on the edge of the pool lived Mr T Toad and his friend Mr Littlefrog. There were little fishes in the pool and snails and beetles and water spiders and other creepy crawly things, but Mr T Toad was far larger than any of them – even Mr Littlefrog looked a very small fellow beside him – and there was no doubt he thought himself far more important, and so did everyone else. Nobody ever thought of calling him just 'Mr Toad'; they always called him 'Mr T Toad'. But no one knew what the T stood for. It might have been Thomas or it might have been Timothy, or even Theophilus; nobody, not even Mr Littlefrog, quite liked to ask him. But the fishes and the beetles and the water snails and spiders all believed it really stood for 'Tremendous'. He was so very proud and grand.

He would sit for hours by the edge of the pool looking at himself in the clear shining water and puffing himself out to look as large as possible. Mr Littlefrog would sit by his side admiring him too, while the fishes popped their heads out of the water to watch, and said to each other, 'How wonderful to have such a great gentleman living amongst us. He must be quite the largest creature in the whole world.' They really believed it. So did Mr T Toad and Mr Littlefrog, and nobody ever came near them to tell them they were wrong. The ground was so marshy and the reeds and rushes so tall and thick that no animals came to drink at the little pool.

So there they all lived together – Mr T Toad, Mr Littlefrog, the beetles, the snails, the water spiders and the fishes – and they would have been as happy as the day was long if it had not been for Mr T Toad's temper. No one could call him a good-tempered toad. You see, he was quite sure that the pool belonged to him, and was meant for him to use as a looking-glass. And if a fish ruffled it, or a water spider ran across it while he was sitting there, or if Mr Littlefrog jumped in 'plop' and made rings all over it, Mr T Toad was very angry indeed. Then he would sit scolding while everyone shivered and shook to listen to him; and

they were all very thankful when he stopped talking and hopped slowly and grumpily away among the bulrush roots and went to sleep.

The times that everyone looked forward to and enjoyed were the days on which Mr T Toad changed his coat. He did not change it very often, because you see his coat was not like yours or mine would be. It grew upon his back and fitted him very comfortably, and his new one grew underneath the old one. When he was ready to change, 'pop' went the old coat and it split, and Mr T Toad wriggled out of it and rolled it up into a neat little ball and *swallowed* it.

But he did not wish the fishes or the beetles or the water spider or snails – or even his friend Mr Littlefrog – to see him half in and half out of his coat. So, when the time came, he always hopped away among the reeds and rushes and spent the day where no one could watch him.

Those were beautiful days. The fishes swam round and round the pool; the water spiders raced across and across; Mr Littlefrog dived in and out; the snails and beetles crawled up and down the stems of the water plants. Everyone played and was happy till Mr T Toad came hopping heavily out of the bulrushes in his fine new coat and sat down to admire himself in the clear water.

Now Mr Littlefrog, as his name tells you, was quite a small fellow. He was a little brown and yellow frog, very slim and quick in the water and very good-natured and kind to everyone. The fishes and the beetles, the water snails and the spiders all liked him. He had plenty of friends to talk to and play with. Sometimes he felt sorry for Mr T Toad. 'Poor fellow!' he said to himself. 'It must be very lonely to be so much greater than everyone else that you have nobody grand enough to talk to.'

Well, one day – it was early in the summer and everyone was feeling happy and bright – Mr T Toad's temper seemed worse than usual. I think it may have been because his coat was growing tight and uncomfortable; it was almost time for him to change it. And as Mr Littlefrog looked at poor sulky Mr T Toad he said to himself, 'A little friendly conversation would do him a world of good. After all, there may be someone to keep him company. I will see what I can do.' And he turned his back on the pleasant little pool and his happy companions and hopped bravely away through the bulrushes to the edge of the marsh. It was just like travelling through a tall forest would be to you or me, and he had never been so far before. Presently he came to thorn bushes and brambles, and it was not easy to find his way through them; but he managed it at last and found himself in a field of grass and tall yellow buttercups. Through the field there ran a little stream which came from the pool where Mr Littlefrog lived. And munching the long grass by the side of the stream was a creature so much larger than Mr T Toad that Mr Littlefrog could hardly believe his eyes. It had a brown and white coat and large brown eyes; it had two horns on its head and a long tail. And as Mr Littlefrog stared at it, the creature lifted its head and said, 'Moo-oo-oo-oo-oo,' and from the other end of the field another creature answered 'Moo-oo-oo-oo-oo!'

It was only a cow, of course, talking to another cow, but it seemed terribly large and noisy to Mr Littlefrog, and he turned round and hopped back to the marsh as quickly as his legs could carry him, with his heart beating very fast and his long legs shaking with fright. He scrambled through the bushes and scuffled through the reeds till he

reached the edge of the pool; and there sat Mr T Toad admiring himself in the clear water while the fishes nudged each other and whispered, 'Keep quiet, he is very cross today.'

'Oh, Mr T Toad! Mr T Toad,' said Mr Littlefrog, all out of breath and in a great hurry, 'I have some wonderful news for you.'

And Mr T Toad, without even turning his head, said, 'Pray do not be so noisy. You disturb me.'

'But Mr T Toad,' said Mr Littlefrog, 'you need not be lonely any longer, for you are not the largest creature in the world. There are others far larger to keep you company.' And all the fishes poked out their heads to listen, and whispered to each other, 'Fancy that!'

But Mr T Toad, still without turning his head, said, 'Pooh!' which was very rude of him. One should not say 'Pooh' to kind people who are trying to tell one things.

'But it is quite true, Mr T Toad,' said Mr Littlefrog. 'I have seen the creature.'

'Pooh!' said Mr T Toad again. 'Is it as large as this?' And he puffed out his sides till he looked like a fat little puppy-dog.

'*Much* larger,' said Mr Littlefrog.

'Rubbish!' said Mr T Toad, and he puffed out his sides till he looked like a football.

'Much, *much* larger, dear Mr T Toad,' said Mr Littlefrog earnestly.

'*Stuff*!' said Mr T Toad very loudly. And he gave a great puff, and '*pop*!' his coat split all down the middle of his back. And a small fish, whose manners were not very good, laughed till it swallowed some water and choked, and then all the other fishes laughed too. They really could not help it.

But Mr T Toad was very angry and very much

upset, and he turned round and hopped away among the bulrush roots as fast as he could go, with his torn coat flapping round him like a mackintosh.

And he never came back! Perhaps he hopped away and found the cow and settled down in the field by the side of the stream; perhaps he found another pond where nobody could laugh at him, and lived there all alone. Perhaps he tried so hard to blow himself up as big as a cow that he blew himself up altogether and flew into little bits. Nobody knows.

Mr Littlefrog and the fishes and the beetles and the water spiders and the snails often used to wonder what had become of him, but they could never really be sorry he had gone. He had been so cross and they were so comfortable without him. So they talked and played their games and chased each other round and round, and ruffled the water just as much as they pleased. And they all lived as happy as the day was long in that pleasant little pool among the reeds and bulrushes, where nobody ever came to trouble them or scold them.

The Tale of the Talkative Sparrow

Once upon a time there lived a sparrow who had her nest upon a great gateway that was the entrance to a King's palace. The gateway was of marble, and it was covered with wonderful carvings of battles and processions and Kings going hunting. It was like a whole picture-book of stories made in stone. Under the gateway people came and went all day. There were the King's soldiers with their shining spears and swords and helmets; there were merchants bringing rich carpets and furs, gold and silver and precious stones to sell to the King. There were ambassadors from far countries with their trains of servants, who came to bring gifts and talk about affairs of state, and there were people of the King's own country who came to tell their troubles and ask for help.

The sparrows looked down from their nests among the carvings and hopped and chirped and watched it all, and told each other in sparrow language what they thought about it.

Sparrows are very noisy little birds, as everybody knows, but one of these sparrows made more noise than any sparrow you or I have ever met. She never stopped talking, and it was all about her own affairs. When anyone else tried to tell her a sparrow-story, she always interrupted then and told one of her own instead; and very often everyone had heard that story so often that nobody wanted to hear it again – but nothing could stop her talking. Just at the time this story begins all her sparrow-children had grown up and flown away. So she had plenty of time to talk. As for her sparrow-husband, I don't know where he was. I expect he had gone somewhere else, because she talked so fast and loud!

Well, one day when Mrs Sparrow was pecking

and scratching in the road to see what she could find to eat, she saw something shining in the dust. It was only a piece of glass, but it sparkled so brightly that Mrs Sparrow thought it must be something very wonderful. She picked it up in her little bill and carried it to her nest. And there she sat, fluttering with excitement and twittering very loud, 'I have a treasure that is greater than the King's! I have a treasure that is greater than the King's! I have a treasure that is greater than the King's!' Her sparrow friends came crowding round to see the wonderful thing.

They pushed and pecked and quarrelled and chirped. Their shrill little voices grew louder and louder, and above them all could be heard Mrs Sparrow shrieking, 'I have a treasure that is greater than the King's.' It was really a terrible noise.

Now this happened just at noon-time, and in the country where Mrs Sparrow lived, everyone rests in the middle of the day because the sun shines so hot and fiercely. The King lay on his bed in his great cool room, and was just dozing off to sleep most comfortably, when the noise began. All the sparrows seemed to be chirping at once, and above them all he could hear, 'Cheep-cheep-*cheep* – cheep-cheep-cheep-cheep-*cheep*,' which of course was Mrs Sparrow's voice. He listened for a little while and hoped they would soon be quiet; but the noise grew louder, and at last the King said very crossly, 'This is *disgraceful*. Tell the Prime Minister to find out what all this fuss is about.'

So the Prime Minister was told that the King could not sleep, and wished him to find out what made the sparrows so noisy. 'Tell the Lord High Chamberlain to attend to the matter at once,' said the Prime Minister, who considered himself far too grand to be concerned with sparrows. And the Lord High Chamberlain told the Butler and the Butler told the Cook and the Cook told the Kitchen-boy. And the Kitchen-boy climbed up the great carved gateway, holding on to the carving with his fingers and toes, and he put his hand into Mrs Sparrow's nest and found the piece of glass. (All the sparrows stopped chattering and flew away when they saw him coming, except Mrs Sparrow, who would not leave her treasure, but even she was quiet.) 'Here is a fine treasure for the King,' said the Kitchen-boy; and he laughed and put the piece of glass in his mouth to keep it safe and climbed down again. Then he gave it to the Cook, and the Cook gave it to the Butler, and the Butler gave it to the Lord High Chamberlain, and the Lord High Chamberlain took it to the Prime Minister, and the Prime Minister laid it on a gold and jewelled tray and carried it to the King.

'This is what the sparrows were making a noise about, your Majesty,' he said. And the King looked at it and said, 'Take it away' (very crossly because he was very sleepy). And he turned over on his other side and said to himself, 'Now I

shall have a little peace and quiet!'

And *then* – would you believe it? – the noise began again, worse than ever. For now Mrs Sparrow had composed a poem about her piece of glass and was shrieking at the top of her voice:

'The King has borrowed my shining treasure,
I lent it to him with pride and pleasure,
No doubt he will pay me back in good measure.'

It was all in sparrow language of course, and I cannot say it was a good poem. But all the other sparrows joined in, some laughing, some cheering, some chattering; and the noise they made was dreadful.

The King sat up, wide awake and very angry. 'Tell the Prime Minister to *catch* that sparrow,' he said. So the Prime Minister sent for the Lord High Chamberlain, the Lord High Chamberlain sent for the Butler, the Butler told the Cook, and the Cook told the Kitchen-boy. And the Kitchen-boy climbed up the great carved gateway once more, holding on with his fingers and toes; and he put out his hand and caught Mrs Sparrow, who was still sitting on her nest, saying her poem at the top of her voice. 'The King wants *you*,' said the

Kitchen-boy. And he held Mrs Sparrow very tight with one hand, and climbed carefully down the carved gateway.

Poor Mrs Sparrow was nearly fainting with fright, but she felt very proud to think the King had sent for her, and she managed to call to her friends, 'The King has sent for me. I will get you all places at Court.' And then the Kitchen-boy carried her into the Palace and gave her to the Cook, and the Cook gave her to the Butler, and the Butler took her to the Lord High Chamberlain, and the Lord High Chamberlain gave her to the Prime Minister. But just as the Prime Minister was going to take her to the King, poor little Mrs Sparrow really did faint right away from fright. And the Prime Minister laid her on a gold and jewelled tray – looking like a dusty little bundle of brown feathers – and took her to the King, and said very grandly, 'The Bird appears to be dead, your Majesty.' And the King said, 'And a very good thing too. Take it away and bury it; and now perhaps I can get a little sleep.'

So the Prime Minister walked out again and said very grandly to the Lord High Chamberlain, 'Take the Bird and bury it'; and the Lord High

Chamberlain told the Butler, and the Butler told the Cook, and the Cook told the Kitchen-boy, and the Kitchen-boy went out into the Palace garden and made a little hole and popped little Mrs Sparrow into it and covered her up. And then he went back into the Palace, and everybody really did get some sleep.

And perhaps you are feeling quite sorry and are thinking that was the end of Mrs Sparrow? But if you do, you are quite wrong.

A Dog had trotted after the Kitchen-boy, wondering if he had anything that was good to eat. And as soon as the Boy had gone, the Dog began to scratch, and he very soon uncovered Mrs Sparrow. But just at that moment Mrs Sparrow opened her little black eyes and sneezed and fluttered her little wings and tried to fly, and found that, instead of being in her own nest, she was lying on the ground with a big Dog looking at her as if he meant to eat her.

She was terribly frightened, but she was really a brave little bird, and a plan came into her little brown head. Instead of trying to get away, she began to talk. 'Oh dear!' said Mrs Sparrow to the Dog, 'are you going to eat me?' 'I certainly am,' said the Dog. 'Dear me!' said Mrs Sparrow, 'how sorry I am for you! My feathers are quite *full* of dust from that nasty hole. I really think you had better wash me first.' 'That seems a good idea,' said the Dog; 'I should never have thought of that.' So he carried Mrs Sparrow to the basin of a fountain and held her in the water till the dust was all washed from her feathers. Poor little Mrs Sparrow didn't like it at all, but she bravely made no fuss. 'Are you going to eat me *now*?' she said, when the Dog had finished. 'I certainly am,' said the Dog. 'But I should taste so *very* nasty and wet,' said Mrs Sparrow; 'hadn't you better dry me

94

first?' 'That is a very good idea,' said the Dog. And he held Mrs Sparrow carefully between his paws whilst the hot sun dried her brown feathers.

By-and-by Mrs Sparrow gave a little cheep and fluffed herself as well as she could. 'I *think* I am quite dry now,' she said, 'but just let me flap my wings and see. It would be a pity to spoil the taste.' 'Certainly it would,' said the Dog, and he moved his paws. And Mrs Sparrow flapped her wings – she flapped her wings and *flew*. Right up to the nest at the top of the great carved gateway she flew, and there she sat and never spoke a word. She had so much to think about!

All her friends knew what had happened. The pigeons that peeped in at the Palace windows and the birds in the Palace garden had told them. And though they were very glad to see her back safe and sound, they really couldn't help laughing at her. And ever after if she talked too importantly and too loudly, somebody was quite sure to say softly, 'Did the King tell you that when you went to Court or did the Dog whisper it in your ear in the Palace garden?' And that always made her feel very quiet!

The Tale of A Tail

It was eleven o'clock at night on Midsummer Eve (which is the twenty-third of June). A fine large moon was sailing high in the sky and Mrs Spriggins' garden looked all silvery in the moonlight. The stones of the garden path shone as white as snow and the grass in the meadow beyond seemed frosted with moonshine.

There was a warm spicy smell from the deep red clove pinks that grew under the kitchen window. Mrs Spriggins could sniff it as she leaned out. But she was not thinking of clove pinks. She was vexed and worried and every few minutes she said to herself, 'Dear, dear, dearie me – wherever can he be?' And she shook her head and looked across the meadow where a big fairy-ring showed quite plain in the moonlight.

'If the Good Folk catch him up to his tricks on Midsummer Eve, he'll get into trouble, so he will,' said Mrs Spriggins. And she leaned out of the window and called very loud, 'Kitty, kitty, kitty! Mr Wickens, Mr Wickens, kitty, kitty-cat!'

'Mr Wickens', as perhaps you have guessed, was the name of Mrs Spriggins' cat. It is an odd name for a cat, but it seemed to suit him very well indeed. He was large and dignified, with a wise, kind face and a satin-smooth dark tabby coat. His tail was long and thick (but not fluffy). Mrs Spriggins liked to draw her hand down his shining back and along his beautiful smooth tail. When she reached the tip of his tail Mr Wickens would stand firmly on his toes and pull softly against her hand, purring with pleasure and delight. They loved each other dearly and they liked each other's ways.

Mr Wickens wore a little leather collar round his neck, like a dog. Fastened to the collar was a tiny tinkling bell; that was to keep him from catching birds. However quietly he crept, the bell tinkled as he moved and the birds heard it and flew away before he reached them. It kept him from catching mice of course, but Mrs Spriggins kept her cat for company, not for mice, so that did not matter.

But on moonlit nights in summer-time Mr Wickens liked to take a walk in the fields, and several times, in spite of his tinkling bell, he had bought back a baby rabbit in his mouth. He carried it quite gently, as a mother-cat carries a kitten, and it was not hurt though it was very frightened. He always trotted in, looking very proud and pleased, and laid the rabbit down in

Mrs Spriggins' kitchen and mewed and purred till Mrs Spriggins came to see what he had brought. She could never make him understand that baby rabbits were no use at all to her. Each time, she had to make a nest in a basket and feed the rabbit till it was old enough to scamper away. But she could not explain to Mr Wickens that he really gave her a good deal of trouble. He was always quite sure that he had brought her a very nice present.

So Mrs Spriggins sat by her kitchen window waiting, and hoping there would not be a baby rabbit that night, because she wanted to go to bed. It was getting very late. She got up from her chair to look at the time and the hands of the tall grandfather clock were almost together. It was very nearly twelve o'clock. 'Dear, dear,' said Mrs Spriggins. But as she leaned out of the window again she heard a little far-off tinkling sound in the stillness, and she said to herself, '*There* he is!'

She could see a little black shadow on the far side of the meadow, slipping along in the moonlight. She called again, 'Mr Wickens, Mr Wickens, kitty, kitty-cat,' and the little black shadow turned and came running across the field, jumping over the big tufts of coarse grass that the cows had left standing here and there. It was Mr Wickens.

'Oh dear,' said Mrs Spriggins, 'he's brought me another.' She could see a little bundle in his mouth. 'Be quick,' she called, 'you naughty cat. It's nearly twelve o'clock.' Just as she spoke the big church clock began to strike, and just as the clock began to strike, Mr Wickens reached the edge of the fairy-ring.

He gave a jump because the grass grew tall and thick round the ring; and as he jumped – he was gone. There was the meadow all white in the moonshine. There was the fairy-ring, like a ring of shadow rather ragged at the edges. But where were Mr Wickens and his baby rabbit? They were nowhere at all!

Mrs Spriggins got up from her chair and ran – all in a hurry – down the garden path, out of the gate and along the little trodden path that led through the meadow beyond. Her long black shadow ran beside her in the moonlight.

She left the path and hurried across to the fairy-ring and stood looking at it. There it was, all quiet and empty; there was not a sound of a tinkling bell, not a shadow, not a purr, not a mew. 'Oh dear, oh dearie me, wherever can he be?' said Mrs Spriggins; and she sat down all in a heap at the edge of the fairy-ring, because quite suddenly she felt all shaky at the knees.

'The Good Folk have taken away my Kitty Wickens,' she said to herself, 'and I don't know what to do about it.'

She was so upset that she was almost crying, and then something touched her face and tickled her nose and made her sneeze instead. It was something velvety and soft as silk. Mrs Spriggins rubbed her nose and looked to see what it could be. Then she rubbed her eyes and looked and looked again. There was no doubt about it. Waving in the moonlight, quite close to her and just outside the fairy-ring, was the tip of Mr Wickens' long smooth tail – only the tip, there was no more of the tail. It ended where the fairy-ring began. Mrs Spriggins put out her hand to seize it, but it whisked away and was gone.

Then she knew what had happened. She had heard her grandmother say that once you stepped inside a fairy-ring on a Midsummer moonlit night, the Good Folk had power over you. If they chose, no one could see you or hear you. There you stayed as long as they willed. They charmed your feet, and they charmed your eyes and your ears. You could only walk and see and hear as the Good Folk chose.

'But they forgot to charm my Kitty Wickens' tail,' said Mrs Spriggins, 'or perhaps it was too long for them. And I'll get him out again, that I will.'

But she could do nothing that night. She waited and watched and waited, but there was never another glimpse of even the tip of Mr Wickens' tail. So at last Mrs Spriggins went back to her cottage and up to bed. At any rate, she knew where her dear cat was, and that was half-way to getting him back again.

She went to bed, but she did not sleep much, as you may guess. She woke very early, while the birds were still whispering to one another, and she lay thinking. Presently she said to herself, 'I'll ask Mrs Featherstone to help me.' And when she had eaten her breakfast, she put on her bonnet and went away down the lane to Mrs Featherstone's cottage.

Mrs Featherstone was large and fat. Mrs

Spriggins was small and thin. But they were very good friends, and Mrs Featherstone thought Mr Wickens was a dear good cat – as indeed he was – so she was quite ready to help. She came along to Mrs Spriggins' cottage at sunset; and as the Midsummer moon came up in the east, large and round and golden-red, Mrs Spriggins and Mrs Featherstone came down the garden path. They each carried a little three-legged wooden stool and they had brought their knitting with them to pass the time away. Mrs Featherstone had a long blue stocking, Mrs Spriggins had a thick grey sock. They could knit by moonlight, or starlight, or any other kind of light. They could even knit in the dark. And moonlight or starlight or dark they meant to stay by the fairy-ring till they saw Mr Wickens' waving tail. 'And *then*,' said Mrs Spriggins, 'we'll see what we'll see!'

So there they sat, on their wooden stools at the edge of the fairy-ring, and their shadows lay beside them, growing shorter and shorter as the moon came creeping up the sky like a golden ball of light. Bats came out of the hollows in the elm-trees and flitted across the field. A great owl came after them, shouting, 'Hoo-hoo. Hoo-hoo-hoo-

hoo-oo-oo.' But there was no sound from the fairy-ring. Nothing moved there, not even a blade of grass.

Ten o'clock struck and still they knitted and waited. Eleven o' clock passed and there was no sign of Mr Wickens or his tail. Twelve o'clock began to strike from the church tower, and as it struck Mrs Spriggins shouted, 'There it is!'

She dropped her knitting and leaned forward and snatched at something that floated in the air just in front of her. It was the tip of Mr Wickens' tail! She held it fast and she could feel him dig in his toes and pull gently against her as he always did when she held his tail. And then – as she leaned forward – the three-legged stool tilted (three-legged stools are very easily upset, you know) and Mrs Spriggins fell, right into the fairy-ring. And what would have been the end of this story if Mrs Featherstone had not been there, I really cannot tell.

There was Mrs Spriggins inside the fairy-ring. She had tight hold of Mr Wickens, it is true; she could feel him as she fell, and she grabbed him with one hand and held him fast. But he seemed as heavy as lead, and her hands and knees and her toes felt full of pins and needles and would not move; and thousands of tiny shining, sparkling wings were dancing before her eyes.

Mrs Spriggins blinked and shut her eyes because they dazzled so, but she held firm and she could feel that Mr Wickens was purring, so she was sure there was nothing to be really afraid of. 'It's just the Good Folk playing tricks on us,' she said to herself. Then she felt a tug and she knew what was happening. Mrs Featherstone had caught her by the arm as she fell and was pulling her out of the fairy-ring. It was a very good thing

that Mrs Featherstone was large and stout and that Mrs Spriggins was small and thin. Mrs Featherstone could see nothing of Mrs Spriggins except her hand, but she held that and pulled and tugged with all her might. And all in a moment – just like a fish out of a pool – out came Mrs Spriggins into the moonlight and out came Mr Wickens too.

And Mrs Featherstone said, '*Well!*' She had no breath to say anything more. And Mrs Spriggins said, '*Well!*' She had no breath either. Then they picked up their three-legged stools and carried

them to the path, quite away from the edge of the fairy-ring. They sat down side by side in the moonlight and looked at each other and nodded their heads, while Mr Wickens walked round them in the moonlight, purring and rubbing against them, saying thank you with all his might.

Mrs Spriggins said, 'Thank you, Mrs Featherstone, my dear.'

Mrs Featherstone said, 'Mrs Spriggins, my dear, I'm sure you're very welcome.'

Then they picked up their three-legged stools and walked across the field and up the garden path to Mrs Spriggins' door. And they each had a large bowl of bread-and-milk, and Mr Wickens – who was very hungry, poor cat – had one too.

It was one o' clock in the morning by the time they had finished their bread-and-milk and their talk about the very strange things that had happened. They said good night at last, and Mrs Spriggins lit the lantern for Mrs Featherstone because the moon was setting and it was really very dark under the trees.

She stood at her cottage door and watched Mrs Featherstone and the lantern go bobbing away down the garden path. Then she shut the door and stroked Mr Wickens, feeling very glad she had him there safe and sound to stroke. Mr Wickens nudged her with his nose, which was *his* way of stroking, and he jumped into the cushioned arm-chair and curled himself up to sleep and Mrs Spriggins climbed the stairs to bed.

What became of the baby rabbit that Mr Wickens carried with him into the fairy-ring, I do not know. But no doubt the Good Folk cared for it and sent it back to its mother. As Mr Wickens never brought another to Mrs Spriggins, they must certainly have explained to him that no really kind cat would steal a baby rabbit. And being a really kind cat, Mr Wickens stole no more. And I expect that pleases you almost as much as it pleased Mrs Spriggins.

The Little Hare and the Tiger

It was ten o'clock on a sunshiny morning – the kind of morning that makes everyone feel happy and cheerful. But no one seemed happy or cheerful in the forest that day. The little hare was sitting in an open space among the bushes at the edge of the wood; he was shaking his head and saying over and over again, '*No*, I shall not go. No,' said the little hare, 'I shall not go. *No*,' said the little hare, very firmly and loudly, 'I *certainly* shall not go.'

By his side sat the jackal, who was saying, 'Oh, do go. Do, *do*, go. Dear hare, dear, kind, beautiful hare, *do* go.' And each time the jackal spoke the little hare shook his head till his ears flapped, and said, 'No, *no*, I shall *not* go.'

Some of the other animals were peeping anxiously out of the bushes. The deer was there, the buffalo, the porcupine, the fox, the pig, the peacock, and many others. They all seemed very worried; and so too would you have been! Now I will tell you what it was all about.

Some time before this story begins a large and hungry tiger had come to live in the forest. Every day he prowled about looking for food, and every day he killed two or three of the animals. He really killed many more than he needed to eat. Everyone was afraid of him, and no one could feel happy or comfortable.

But one day the jackal had a bright idea – at least it seemed bright to *him*. He called a meeting of the animals and told them of his plan. 'Suppose,' said the jackal, 'we promised to send one animal every day for the tiger's dinner. Then the rest of us would be safe that day, for he would not go roaring though the forest killing everyone he met.' (And the jackal thought in his cunning head, 'We could send all the small animals first, and then *I*

112

should be safe for a very long time.')

The other animals agreed. The tiger agreed. He was growing fat and lazy, and it saved him trouble. Everyone was pleased except the little hare. When they told him he was to run along and be the tiger's dinner, he was not pleased at all. And I really do not wonder – do you?

So now you know why everyone in the forest was so worried that beautiful sunshiny morning. The animals were all afraid that if the tiger was kept waiting for his dinner he might come to fetch it and perhaps fetch several of them as well.

But nobody could persuade the little hare to go, and nobody wanted to go instead of him. The sun crept up and up the sky till it was shining just overhead, which meant it was twelve o'clock. All the little hare would say when they told him how badly he was behaving, was, 'Don't disturb me; I am thinking.' And by this time the tiger could plainly be heard roaring with rage, but luckily he was too fat and lazy to trouble to leave his den.

However, twelve o'clock in the forest is a hot and sleepy time of day. Presently the tiger was quiet; even the jackal stopped talking, and most of the animals were having a little midday nap. So they were all very much surprised when, just as the shadows of the rocks and trees had grown large enough to show that it was one o'clock, the little hare suddenly gave a jump and a shout. 'I'm off,' he said. And off he went, running so fast that it really seemed as if he would fall head over heels. And when the animals saw which way he was running they all gave a great sigh, or a squeak, or a grunt of relief, and began to look about to see what they could find for their dinners.

Where do you think the little hare was going? You will be very surprised to hear that he ran straight to the cave where the tiger lived. He was in such a hurry that when he got there it seemed as if he couldn't stop himself, and he almost tumbled into the tiger's paws. But not quite into them; he was very careful to keep just out of reach. The tiger was very angry at having been kept waiting so long, but he had been dozing and was still only half awake. So instead of putting out his big paw to catch the little hare, he growled, 'Come here, you miserable little creature, and don't tumble about like that. What do you mean by being so late?'

The little hare began to sob. (He was panting so

114

much that it was easy to pretend.) 'Oh, my lord
tiger,' he said, 'I am so thin, so very thin, and my
brother was so fat.'

'Then why didn't they send him instead?'
roared the tiger.

'They did,' said the little hare; 'they did. Oh,
they did. But the other tiger got him first.'

'Who-oo-oo-oo-oo?' roared the tiger.

'The other tiger,' sobbed the little hare, 'who
lives in the hole among the bushes near by.'

'Take me to him,' roared the tiger; 'I will teach
him to eat my dinner and leave a miserable thing
like you.'

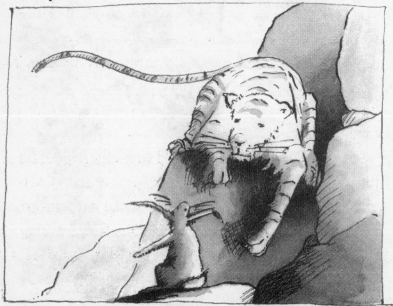

'Very well,' said the little hare, still sobbing. 'Very well. Come this way, my lord. Come quietly, and I will take you to his den.'

And the little hare led the tiger to a narrow path which wound in and out among the tall grass. Tigers are like cats, they cannot see very well in bright sunlight, and the tiger blinked and peered this way and that. Suddenly the little hare darted into some bushes. 'This way, my lord,' he said, 'this way.' The tiger leaped over the bushes and landed in a little open space. There was a deep hole, by the side of which stood the little hare. 'Here is his den, my lord,' he said, in a trembling voice. 'Oh! Oh! Oh! I am so frightened. Let me stand close beside you!'

The tiger went to the edge and looked. There, looking up at him out of the hole, was the face of a very angry tiger, and beside him was a very frightened hare.

'*Give me my dinner,*' roared the tiger, and he jumped – and splash! he went, down and down and down. And he never came up any more. For the hole was a deep well, filled with water as clear and shining as a looking-glass, and the tiger with whom he was so angry was really

117

his greedy self with the little hare at his side.

As for the little hare, he went scampering back to the open space where this story begins. And there he found a hollow log and climbed upon it, and he drummed with his strong hind legs and sang:

'Come! Come! Come!
I beat upon the drum
Pr-r-rump, pr-r-rump, pr-r-rump,
I saw the tiger jump.
Down in the well he fell,

As I am here to tell.
Pr-r-rump, pr-r-rump, pr-r-rump,
I saw the tiger jump!'

The animals came creeping out of the bushes to listen, and when the little hare had sung it all through, they all joined in and sang joyfully in chorus:

'Down in the well he fell;
The hare is here to tell.'

till they were all quite hoarse with singing. And then they all went happily home to sleep.

The Tale of Brave Augustus

Once upon a time an old woman whose name was Mrs Popple lived in a little white cottage among wide green fields. The cottage had a garden where Mrs Popple grew potatoes and onions and cabbages and carrots, and there was a border of flowers each side of the path that led to the garden gate. Beyond the gate there was a little pond with reeds and rushes by its edge; and on the pond lived Augustus, Mrs Popple's large white gander. Once there had been two geese upon the pond, for Augustus had a wife who was named Augusta. But Augusta had died, and since then Augustus had been all alone.

Mrs Popple was very kind to him. She fed him well (in fact, she fed him so well that Augustus was far too fat to fly). When she called to him, Augustus would come waddling to meet her, with his long neck stretched out, all ready to take nice bits of fat and soaked bread and juicy cabbage. She often chatted to him, and sometimes when she walked in the fields on spring evenings to look for early primroses or violets in the hedges, Augustus would go with her. He gabbled while Mrs Popple talked, and while Mrs Popple picked flowers Augustus picked slugs and snails and fresh green blades of young grass; so they both enjoyed their walk.

But in spite of all this, Augustus was sometimes very lonely. He longed for a real companion.

Mrs Popple had two cats; their names were Daisy and Dora. She had two rabbits; their names were James and John. She had quite a family of chickens and two hives of bees. All her pets had companions except poor Augustus; and though she and Augustus talked to each other in their own way, Augustus often felt he could say much more if he had another goose to speak to.

One fine evening in April Mrs Popple came

down her garden path. Spring really had come at last. Her clumps of double daffodils had pointed green buds and big yellow flowers. Her red and yellow polyanthuses were all in bloom. There were white violets and blue violets tucked in among the stones by the gate, and the fat green shoots on her lilac tree were all unfolding. The grass smelled fresh and the wind was soft. 'It's a pleasant evening,' said Mrs Popple, 'I shall take a little walk.'

She called to Augustus and he came sailing to the edge of the pond. The bank was very low on the side nearest the cottage, and Augustus stepped out and waddled after Mrs Popple. Daisy and Dora, the cats, came a little way with them, and then Mrs Popple and Augustus went on alone. Mrs Popple was stooping down to pick primroses in a little lane when she noticed that Augustus was behaving very oddly. He was trying to stand on tip-toe (and you know that his feet were not really the right shape for that). He was flapping his wings and stretching his long neck and calling 'Ga-ga-ga' very loudly.

'Whatever is the matter, Augustus dear?' said Mrs Popple.

She looked up at the sky as Augustus was looking, and high overhead she saw three great birds come flying – three big grey birds, with wide wings and long stretched-out necks.

'Oh!' said Mrs Popple, 'it's the wild geese. There they go, flying north with the spring, to make their nests. Don't you try to go with them and leave me, Augustus dear.'

Augustus said 'Ga-ga-ga' and flapped his wings again. The wild geese took no notice of his calling. They flew on fast and steadily. But some way behind them came another goose. It was flying slowly. It seemed very tired, and it was getting slower every minute and flying lower and lower still.

'Augustus,' said Mrs Popple, 'that goose must have hurt its wing. It won't fly far. I shouldn't be surprised if it came down in the Marsh. I hope the fox won't get it, poor thing.'

But of course all Augustus could say to her was 'Ga-ga-ga' again. It was really very awkward for him to have no one really to talk to when he had so much to say. For Augustus was full of excitement to think that another goose was so near. Perhaps if I could find her, she would stay on the pond with

me, he thought. And he made up his mind to go and look for the goose that very night.

Late that evening, Mrs Popple stood at her garden gate calling for Augustus. She called and called, but no Augustus came waddling across the field. At last Mrs Popple shut the door of the shed where Augustus always slept with James and John and she went indoors. She went to bed very worried. She was certain that something had happened to her dear Augustus. She scarcely slept all night, and before the sun was up next morning she stood by her garden gate calling and calling again.

You and I know what had happened of course, but Mrs Popple did not. Augustus had gone. He had gone to look for the goose that was hurt. He did not know where the Marsh was, but he was determined to find out. (Perhaps I had better explain, in case you do not know, that a Marsh is a place where the ground is soft and wet, with reeds and rushes and water-plants growing on it.)

When he came back with Mrs Popple from their walk together, he swam round and round the pond, thinking about it all. When Mrs Popple went indoors to get her supper Augustus came out of the pond and hurried away, across the field.

He could go quite fast for a short distance because he flapped his wings and that helped him to run. But he soon got out of breath and had to go more slowly.

It was growing dark by that time and Augustus had never been out alone after dusk. But the sky looked very high and wide and clear; two or three bright stars were twinkling and there was a silver-shining half-moon. 'Plenty of light to see by,' said Augustus bravely to himself, and he waddled on with his little black shadow beside him in the moonlight.

He was just squeezing through a gap in a hedge when suddenly a big brown hare jumped up right in front of him out of a ditch. It frightened Augustus terribly, and he had just opened his beak to say 'Ga-ga-ga' very loudly when he remembered that he had better not make a noise, or Mrs Popple might find him and drive him home. So he only said, in a rather panting voice, 'Please could you tell me the way to the Marsh? I want to find the goose that has hurt her wing.'

'Certainly I can tell you; I saw the goose myself,' said the hare. 'Shall I come with you? I might be some use.'

'Yes, do come,' said Augustus. So they went on together with their two little black shadows in the moonlight, and Augustus felt very glad to have the hare for company.

They were going very quietly and carefully across the grass when a very loud 'Buzz-zz-zz,' just beside his yellow foot, made poor Augustus jump again. It was a bumble-bee that had stayed out too late. He was sitting on a dandelion, cold and cross and sleepy, and he was afraid that Augustus might gobble him up with his yellow bill. But when Augustus and the hare explained where they were going, the bumble-bee said, 'I saw the goose too. Shall I come with you? I might be some use.'

'Yes, do come,' said Augustus. He could not quite see what use the bumble-bee could be; but he said to himself, 'Every little helps.' So he let the bumble-bee crawl up his yellow bill and on to his feathery white head. It was tickly for Augustus, but the feathers were warm and comfortable for the bumble-bee. So they went on together with their three little black shadows in the moonlight. The bumble-bee's shadow made a little bump on the top of Augustus's head.

Presently they came to a high green bank with a gate in it. The gate stood open, and they were just going to pass through when something small and fluffy and noisy bounced out of a hole in the bank and hit poor Augustus in one eye. 'Chit-chit-chit-cheep-cheep-chitter-chee,' it said in a very shrill voice. Augustus thought that some fierce creature was trying to bite his head off. But it was only a little brown Jenny-wren that had waked up suddenly in a fright when she heard them coming. And when they explained where they were going, Jenny-wren said, 'I saw the goose, too. Shall I come with you?'

'Yes, do come,' said Augustus. Jenny-wren perched herself on his tail feathers, and they went on together with their four little black shadows in the moonlight. Jenny-wren's shadow made a lump on the end of Augustus's tail.

By this time they were going downhill to the Marsh. They were passing some bushes when there was a very loud sneeze, so loud that Augustus jumped with fright and almost ran away. But it was only a little old brown donkey who was standing half asleep in the shadow. They told him where they were going and he said,

'I know where the goose is. She is hiding in the Marsh. Shall I come with you?'

'Yes, do come,' said Augustus, and they went on together with their five black shadows in the moonlight. The donkey went first, and the hare and Augustus with the bumble-bee and Jenny-wren followed close behind him.

They were close to the edge of the Marsh when suddenly the donkey stopped. He put his head down; his long brown ears stood straight up and then they pointed forward. Augustus and the hare peeped out from behind the donkey's tail. They crept forward to see what he was looking at. He was standing at the edge of a wide ditch, staring at a big fox that was creeping along in the shadow. They had come so softly over the grass that the fox had not heard them. His ears were pricked, his eyes were shining, his bushy tail trailed behind him. Quickly and quietly he was crawling down to the Marsh to catch the goose that had hurt her wing.

And all at once Augustus quite forgot about being frightened. 'Ga-ga-ga,' he cried and flapped his wings. It surprised the hare so much that he jumped straight into the ditch, right on top of the

fox. Augustus jumped too. He caught the fox's tail with his strong beak and pinched and tweaked with all his might. The fox snarled and turned to snap at Augustus. 'Buzz-zz-zz,' said the bumble-bee and bumped the fox on his nose; while Jenny-wren shrieked 'Chee-chee-chee-chee-e-e-p' and flew straight into his eyes, and the donkey brayed and brayed with all his might.

The fox could not think what had happened to him. He had never been so frightened in all his life. He gave a wriggle and a jump and the next minute he was out of the ditch and running across the field. He ran and ran, and never stopped running till he was safe in his den in the wood; and he stayed there the rest of the night.

But Augustus did not stop to see what the fox was doing. He could hear a flapping and a fluttering and an anxious goose-voice calling. He spread his wings wide and ran. The goose with the lame wing was calling from the Marsh where she had been trying to hide among some clumps of big yellow marsh marigolds and tall dead reeds and bulrushes. Her wing was too stiff to fly, and the fox would have caught her quite easily.

Augustus ran to her and stroked her with his

bill. He talked to her in goose-language, and told her she was safe and that he would take care of her and take her to his home. The grey goose talked to him and told him all her troubles and how a man had shot at her and hurt her wing. By and by they had a little sleep; the bumble-bee buzzed to itself in a yellow marsh marigold, and Jenny-wren chirped sleepily in a willow tree, and the donkey and the hare nibbled grass.

So they all spent the rest of the night together, feeling happy and proud and contented, and in the morning Augustus thanked his kind friends and they all set out across the fields to their homes.

Mrs Popple was standing at her garden gate. She had been there since daybreak, as you know, calling for Augustus. She was beginning to feel most sadly sure that she would never see him again. She watched the sun rise out of a grey mist, she saw the dewdrops sparkle and twinkle all over the green grass. It was a pretty morning, but she could not feel happy when Augustus was lost. 'Au-gus-tus, Augustus!' she called again and again. And then all of a sudden she stopped. 'I do believe I hear his voice!' said Mrs Popple.

She listened and she heard it quite plainly. Augustus was talking to the grey goose; and then she saw them both. They squeezed through the hole in the hedge and came stepping proudly and happily across the field in the sunshine.

'Bless me,' said Mrs Popple, 'my brave Augustus! He's found the goose that was hurt and brought it home.'

She ran into the house and came out with a pan full of lovely scraps and soaked bread and mutton fat, greens and a large crumbled bit of cake (which she put in extra because she was so happy). She put the pan down and Augustus and the grey

goose scurried to it, and emptied it in a great hurry. They were both very hungry. Then they waddled to the pond, and soon they were washing themselves and tidying their feathers as if they had both lived there all their lives.

The grey goose's wing never quite got well again. It was always too stiff to fly far. But she did not seem to mind. She settled down on Mrs Popple's pond, and she and Augustus brought up family after family of fluffy yellow goslings. Augustus never felt lonely again, and he and the grey goose loved each other dearly as long as they lived. So I think you might say that the end of this story is 'They lived happily ever after.'

THE Berenstain BEAR SCOUTS

in

Giant Bat Cave

by Stan & Jan Berenstain

Illustrated by Michael Berenstain

Hippo

Scholastic Children's Books,
Commonwealth House, 1–19 New Oxford Street,
London WC1A 1NU, UK
a division of Scholastic Ltd
London ~ New York ~ Toronto ~ Sydney ~ Auckland

First published in the US by Scholastic Inc., 1995
Published in the UK by Scholastic Ltd, 1996

ISBN 0 590 13903 7

Typeset by Rapid Reprographics
Printed by Cox & Wyman Ltd, Reading, Berks.

10 9 8 7 6 5 4 3 2 1

• Contents •

THE
Berenstain
BEAR
SCOUTS
in
GIANT BAT CAVE

• Chapter 1 •
One for All, and All for One

The Bear Scouts met with Scout Leader
Jane about once a month. They usually
met on merit badge business. That's what
today's meeting was about.

"We've decided to try for the Good
Government Merit Badge, Scout Leader,"
said Scout Brother.

"Goo goo," said Sister.

"I should know better than to ask," said
Jane, "but why are you talking baby talk?"

The troop grinned.

"That's slang for 'good government',"
said Scout Fred.

1

Scout Leader Jane almost smiled, but kept herself from doing so. The troop liked to make jokes. Especially Scout Sister, who was a bit of a smarty. But Jane thought it best to be serious. She was not only a scout leader, she was a teacher at Bear Country School as well.

In fact, both Scout Sister and Scout Lizzy were in her class. The other two members of the troop were Scout Brother and Scout Fred. They were two years above Sister and Lizzy.

But girl or boy, younger or older, they were all scouts together. "One for all, and all for one" was their slogan. It came from a book Scout Fred had read – it was called *The Bear Musketeers*. It was about some soldiers from olden times. They would cross their swords and shout, "One for all, and all for one!" Then they would rush off to rescue a princess or slay a dragon.

But there weren't any princesses in Bear

Country, or any dragons – at least as far as anyone knew.

Nor did the Bear Scouts have swords to cross. But they crossed other things when they said their slogan – like straws once, when they were having milkshakes at the Burger Bear, or rulers or pencils at school, or even sticks when they were gathering wood for a campfire.

Brother, Sister, Fred, and Lizzy liked being Bear Scouts. They liked having Jane as their leader, too. One of the reasons was that she trusted them. The scouts knew that other scout leaders fussed about everything their troops wanted to do. But not Jane. She didn't even know where the troop's secret clubhouse was. The only person besides the scouts who did know was Farmer Ben. That was because the scouts' secret clubhouse was an old chicken coop that Farmer Ben wasn't using for chickens any more.

From the outside it still looked like a broken-down old chicken coop. It looked much better from the inside. It wasn't fancy. There wasn't much furniture, and what there was was very simple. The table was made of an old door. There were two old kitchen chairs that Farmer Ben had given them. But mostly the scouts sat in the small grandstand they had made from

the chicken roost. They had done this by
nailing boards to the poles that the
chickens had roosted upon.

The scouts had been able to keep their
clubhouse secret because nobody ever saw
them going into it. Farmer Ben had built
the chicken coop on to an old hollow tree.
The scouts went in through the hollow
tree. There were bushes around the opening, so the scouts were able to slip in without ever being seen.

It hadn't been easy turning the chicken
coop into a clubhouse. The scouts had been
very happy when Farmer Ben told them
they could have the place. But when they
first went in, they were shocked. It was
the dirtiest place any of them had ever
seen – and the smelliest! At first they
couldn't stop yelling "Phew!" over and over
again. Their eyes watered and their noses
burned. But they rolled up their sleeves
and went to work. They carried out bag

after bag of chicken feathers. They scrubbed and scrubbed and scrubbed. After a lot of cleaning up and fixing up, the place began to look like a real clubhouse.

You'd hardly know that it had once been a chicken coop, except for two things: It still had a funny smell on rainy days, and once in a while a chicken would show up and make itself at home.

• Chapter 2 •

The Honour Wall

One wall of the Bear Scouts' clubhouse was special. They called it their honour wall. On it were the merit badges the troop had already earned. There were three of them: a Good Deed Merit Badge, a Water Safety Merit Badge, and a Recycling Merit Badge.

They had earned the first by helping the Widder McGrizz when she was ill with the flu. They had done her grocery shopping and other helpful things. They had earned the second by learning the dead bear's float, the doggie paddle, and the sidestroke. They had earned the third merit badge by putting paper, glass, and metal in different bins for collection.

The three merit badges were pinned to a ribbon that was tacked to the honour wall. It was a long ribbon. There was room on it for more merit badges.

But the most important thing on the honour wall was the Bear Scout Oath. This is what it looked like, and this is what it said:

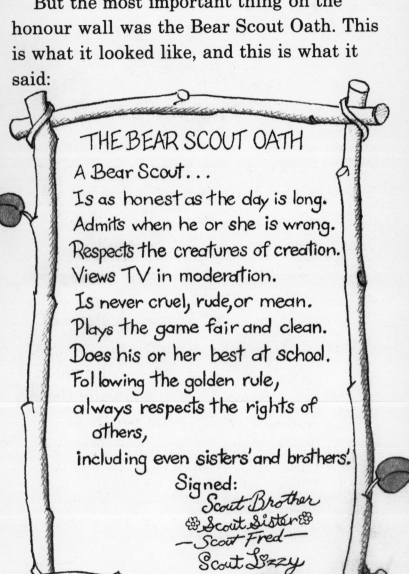

THE BEAR SCOUT OATH

A Bear Scout...
Is as honest as the day is long.
Admits when he or she is wrong.
Respects the creatures of creation.
Views TV in moderation.
Is never cruel, rude, or mean.
Plays the game fair and clean.
Does his or her best at school.
Following the golden rule,
always respects the rights of
others,
including even sisters' and brothers'.

Signed:
Scout Brother
Scout Sister
Scout Fred
Scout Lizzy

• Chapter 3 •
A Letter for Gus

The Bear Scout Oath hung on the wall of
Scout Leader Jane's office as well. It was
exactly the same, except for one thing.
There were five names at the bottom
instead of four. The fifth name was that of
Scout Leader Jane.

Jane was proud of her troop. One of the
things she was most proud of was the way
they did things on their own. Take merit
badges, for instance. They got them the
old-fashioned way: They *earned* them.

Leader Jane got up from her desk and
took a book from the shelves. It was the
Official Bear Scout Handbook. "Hmm,"
she said. "Let's see what you have to do to

earn the Good Government Merit Badge."

Jane read aloud, "'The Good Government Badge can be earned in a number of ways: one, by studying the workings of government; two, by helping during an election; three, by interviewing at least three important government officials. The troop will then report to the troop leader. The leader will decide whether or not to award the Good Government Merit Badge.'"

The scouts thought it over. They couldn't choose "helping during an election" because it wasn't election time. They couldn't interview three important government officials because Beartown didn't have three important officials. It had only two: Mayor Horace J. Honeypot and Chief of Police Bruno.

"I suppose studying the workings of government is all that's left," said Scout Sister. "But how are we going to do that?"

"You will do that by going to an important meeting at Town Hall this evening,"

said Jane. She took a piece of Bear Scout
letter paper and began writing.

"Hey, wait a minute," said Scout Fred. "I
know about that meeting. My parents are
going to it. But they couldn't find a bear-
sitter because everybody else is going to
that meeting, too."

"Our parents are having the same
problem," said Scout Brother.

"Mine too," said Scout Lizzy.

"Well," said Jane, "they won't need bear-
sitters, because you'll be going, too. They
don't usually allow cubs at town meetings.
So here's a letter telling Gus the doorkeeper
to let you in. He was in my class when he
was a cub. He knows better than to not
do what I say."

"Leader Jane?" said Sister.

"Yes, Scout Sister."

"What's this big important meeting
about?"

"You'll find that out soon enough," said
Jane.

• Chapter 4 •
No Cubs Allowed

The Bear Scouts had never seen such a crowd. Everybody who was anybody was going into the meeting. Everybody except cubs, of course. The Bear Scouts were the only cubs in sight.

"Gosh," said Lizzy, "I hope they let us in."

"This letter from Scout Leader Jane should do it," said Brother. But he was just as nervous as Lizzy. Their parents had already gone into the meeting. So had Brother and Sister's grandparents.

"Just a minute, please. Where do you think you're going? This is a meeting for grown-ups."

It was Gus, the doorkeeper. He was so big that the scouts could hardly see past him into the hall.

"W-well," said Brother, "we're trying for our Good Government Merit Badges and—"

"Show him the letter," said Sister.

The letter was short and to the point. It said, "To Whom It May Concern – especially Gus the doorkeeper, who used to be in my class. Please admit my Bear Scout troop. They are on official business." It was signed "Scout Leader Jane".

"Well, I don't know," said Gus, reading the letter. The bears lined up outside began to shout, "Let us in!" and "What's the hold-up?"

"What beems to see the bubble, Gus? Er – what seems to be the trouble?"

It was the voice of Mayor Horace J. Honeypot himself. It was easy to tell because Mayor Honeypot often got the fronts and the backs of his words mixed up.

Mayor Honeypot took the letter from Gus and read it. "Let them in, my all beans – er, by all means! Why, bubs – er, cubs – are our country's future!"

The scouts did not like all the fuss. They quickly found seats in the back row of the crowded hall.

"You know, we still don't know what this big important meeting is about," said Fred.

"That may be," said Sister. "But I'll tell you this: It's got to be about something a little strange. Because *look*!" She pointed to the stage.

"Good grief!" said Brother. "Ralph Ripoff! Right up there on the stage! And shaking hands with the mayor!"

The scouts really couldn't be blamed for being surprised, even shocked. Ralph was famous around Beartown. A better word would be "infamous", which means famous in a bad way. The kindest thing to be said about Ralph was that he couldn't exactly be trusted. A not-so-kind thing to

17

say was that Ralph was a no-good, low-down crook.

Maybe the best way to tell you about Ralph Ripoff is to repeat what some of his fellow bears said about him.

Here's what Grizzly Gramps, Brother and Sister's grandfather, had to say: "Ralph reminds me of one of those hot-air balloons: no visible means of support – except the hot air he's full of."

Papa had a different idea about Ralph: "I like Ralph. Sure, he's smooth and tricky. You just have to watch him, that's all."

This is what Mama had to say about Ralph: "I was taught that if you couldn't say something good about someone, you shouldn't say anything. So I won't say anything."

• Chapter 5 •

Something Wonderful

But no matter what Gramps, Papa, and Mama thought about Ralph, there he was up there on the stage. He and the mayor were shaking hands like old friends.

The mayor tested the sound system. "One-two, one-two," he said. As he did so, a big movie screen came down behind him.

"I wid you all belcome – er, bid you all welcome!" said the mayor. "I have called this cheating – er, meeting – to talk about a wonderful new project. And now, leading citizen, Mr Ralph Ripoff . . ."

"Leading citizen?" whispered Scout Brother.

"Doesn't he mean *leading crook*?" whispered Scout Sister.

". . . will sell you – er, tell you – about something that will be a great boon to Beartown . . ."

"What's a 'boon'?" whispered Sister.

"*Boon*," whispered Fred, who read the dictionary for fun. "*Something good, something of value*."

". . . something that will bring much happiness to the citizens of Beartown. And something," the mayor went on, "that will also bring *much money* to the citizens of Beartown."

There was a buzz in the audience when they heard the word "money".

"And so it is with much pleasure that I give you my great and good friend, Mr Rip Ralphoff – er, Ralph Ripoff!"

As Ralph stood up, the lights went down. A spotlight shone on Ralph. He clicked a clicker and said, "First slide, please."

A picture filled the screen. It was a picture of a place everybody knew about.

"It's Giant Bat Cave!" said Scout Fred.

"Why is he showing us a picture of that yucky place?" said Sister. Others in the hall were wondering the same thing.

"That's right," said Ralph. "It's Giant Bat Cave. A nasty, filthy place if ever there was one. Filled with thousands of nasty, filthy bats."

As Ralph spoke he clicked his clicker and more pictures came on to the screen. There was a picture of the cave with a thick cloud of bats pouring out of its mouth.

"Ooh!" said Sister. "Bats give me the shivers."

There was a picture of what could have been the inside of a great dragon's mouth with rows and rows of terrible teeth. Of course, it wasn't. It was the inside of Giant Bat Cave, and the "teeth" were stalactites and stalagmites.

"And now," said Ralph, "Ripoff Productions presents . . . *something wonderful*! New slide, please!"

When the next slide came on the screen, the crowd couldn't believe its eyes. It showed the outside of Giant Bat Cave, but it wasn't spooky and gloomy any more. It was bright and beautiful. There was a great golden sign that said WELCOME TO RALPH'S CAVERAMA – THE UNDERGROUND WONDERLAND.

The next picture showed the inside. It was even more beautiful. It no longer looked like a dragon's mouth with terrible teeth. It looked like . . . well, an *underground wonderland*! There were coloured lights, all kinds of fun rides, and more gift shops and food stands than you could count.

• Chapter 6 •

All Those in Favour, Say "Aye!"

At first a hush came over the crowd. As the lights came up, so did the crowd. They stood as one and cheered and cheered. The Bear Scouts joined in. Except for Scout Lizzy, who was *not* standing or cheering.

"What a great idea!" shouted Brother. "An underground theme park!"

Getting cheered was a new thing for Ralph. He was more used to getting chased down the road by folks he had tricked or cheated. Ralph liked being cheered. He smiled and raised his hands over his head.

Mayor Honeypot looked very pleased

too. He held out his hands to shush the crowd. "Now, before putting this to a vote," he said, "the law says we have to take comments. Yes, Squire Grizzly. Do you have a comment?"

Squire Grizzly was Beartown's richest citizen. He owned supermarkets, petrol stations, a bank, and a TV station.

"I think Mr Ripoff's project is a good idea," said the Squire. "It will bring visitors from all over Bear Country. It will be very good for business. Lady Grizzly and I will vote 'yes'."

Many leading citizens spoke in favour of Ralph's project. Max Bearskin, owner of the Bearskin Arms Motel, thought it was a fine idea. "It will keep my motel rooms filled all year round," he said.

Brad Bruin of Bruin, Bruin, Bruin, and Grizzly, Beartown's leading law firm, offered to draw up the legal papers – for a fee, of course.

The audience was excited about Ralph's

project. Papa Bear, who was a woodworker, was very excited. He turned to Mama and said, "See, I told you Ralph wasn't such a bad guy. That Caverama's going to need a lot of woodwork."

"Perhaps," said Mama, "Ralph will let us put in a little quilt shop." Mama's quilting club raised money for Beartown Hospital.

"Of course he will," said Papa. "I'll speak to him about it."

"Maybe I could put in a vegetable stand!" said Farmer Ben.

Grizzly Gramps had a very different idea about Ralph's project. "I can't stand this any longer," he said. "Somebody's got to warn these folks. The only one that's gonna make money out of Ralph's Caverama is Ralph. Ripoff's his name, and rippin' folks off is his game. So I gotta speak my mind." He started to stand to have his say, but Gran stopped him.

"Hush up, you old grouch!" said Gran.

Her hobby was reading palms and telling fortunes. "Maybe Ralph will let me set up a little fortune-telling booth."

Grizzly Gramps just groaned.

Just about everybody, except Gramps, was talking about some way of being a part of Ralph's Caverama. But nobody at that meeting had given a single thought to what might happen to the thousands of bats when their home was turned into an underground theme park. Nobody, that is, except Bear Scout Lizzy.

"All right. Let's quiet down now," said the mayor. "It's vime for a tote – er, time for a vote. All those in favour of turning Giant Bat Cave into a wonderful money-making underground theme park, raise your hands and say 'aye!'"

Hundreds of hands shot up. The shouts of "aye!" shook the building.

Mayor Honeypot looked out over the sea of raised hands. It was almost like counting votes in the next election.

"All right," said the mayor. "There's really no need to bother, but by law I have to ask all those opposed to raise their hands and say 'nay!'"

A single "nay!" sounded in the hall. It was a small voice, but it could be heard clearly in the silence. But whose voice was it? It couldn't be Grampa's.

Everybody looked around. But they couldn't see the naysayer.

So that she could be seen, Bear Scout Lizzy stood on her chair and said it again. "Nay!" she said loud and clear.

Scouts Brother, Sister, and Fred looked at Lizzy. They were just as surprised as everybody else.

Mayor Honeypot was surprised and

very annoyed. He looked out into the
hall. "Why, as I live and breathe,
it's a bub – er, cub. Who let that bub – er,
cub – in here?"

"You did, Mr Mayor," said Gus, the
doorkeeper.

"Well, don't let it happen again," said
the mayor. "As for you, young lady, you're a
bub – er, cub. And cubs don't vote!"

"That may be, sir," said Lizzy in a small
but strong voice. "But somebody has to
speak for the bats. They will be homeless
if you—"

"All right, you cubs, out of here!" said
Gus. He pushed them out the door.

• Chapter 7 •

Nature's Creatures, Great and Small

Scouts Brother, Sister, and Fred shouldn't have been surprised when Lizzy stood up for the bats. They knew that Lizzy had a special feeling for animals. "Nature's creatures, great and small, nature's creatures, one and all" was a favourite saying of Lizzy's. It showed how she felt about animals.

While the members of the Bear Scout troop were "one for all and all for one", each scout was his or her own person with his or her own special talents. Brother was pretty much of a straight arrow and a natural leader. Scout Sister had lots of spunk.

Scout Fred was smart as a whip. And Scout Lizzy had this amazing way with animals – all kinds of animals. Butterflies would alight on her finger. Squirrels would bring her acorns. Lizzy could even pet a skunk without getting skunked.

But her fellow scouts didn't know she had a thing for bats. Now they had upset the mayor and got themselves kicked out of a big important meeting. How would they earn their Good Government Merit Badges now?

The scouts were talking about it as they walked home.

"Look, Lizzy," said Sister, "butterflies, squirrels, even skunks are one thing – but bats? Yuck!"

Lizzy didn't say anything. But as they walked along in the evening, she held up her hand. Fireflies began to land on it. After a while Lizzy's hand was almost like a lamp lighting their way.

"Well, I for one think Lizzy's got a point," said Fred. "Those bats have lived in

Giant Bat Cave for hundreds, even thousands, of years."

"Yes," said Sister, "but Ralph's Caverama looked really cool. And besides, you heard what he said. How bats are filthy and all."

"I happen to know that's not true," said Fred. "They're not filthy. They're at least as clean as Ralph."

"Maybe so," said Sister, "but they are weird. I mean, they like to hang upside down."

"What's the harm in that?" said Fred. "Being against somebody just because they like to hang upside down is plain prejudice."

"I suppose so," said Sister. "What do you think, Brother?"

Brother didn't answer. He just walked along deep in thought.

"Goodbye, little friends," said Lizzy. She held up her glowing hand. Her firefly friends flew off in every direction. Then

Lizzy turned to her fellow scouts. "Dirty or clean, upside down or right side up," she said, "taking away the bats' home is totally, totally wrong. And we have to stop it from happening. What do *you* think, Brother?"

"I agree with you," said Brother. "The trouble is, bats don't vote."

"Maybe bats don't vote," said Fred. "But they do something just as important. They eat bugs. Zillions of 'em. Why, if it weren't for bats . . ."

"That's right," said Brother. "Yes, it's all part of planet ecology. I know – why don't we take this problem to Professor Actual Factual over at the Bearsonian?"

"It's a deal," said Fred. "We'll go over there first thing in the morning."

That's when they heard someone shouting. "Hey! Wait for me!"

It was Grizzly Gramps. The scouts slowed down so Gramps could catch up.

• Chapter 8 •

Gramps Remembers

"Hi, Gramps," said the scouts.

"Hi. I was proud of you cubs back there standin' up to Ralph and the mayor. Ralph's got folks' tongues hangin' out for all that money. It's like old J. P. Bearnum said: There's a sucker born every minute. And Ralph had a whole town hall full of 'em back there."

"Gramps, we were just talking about how important bats are to the ecology," said Brother. "Do you have any idea how Ralph can be stopped?"

"Well," said Gramps, "I'm not much of an *ec*-ologist. I'm more of a *Ralph*-ologist. I think the only way to stop Ralph is to beat him at his own game. You've got to trick him, fool him, *scare him off.*"

Gramps looked back. Gran and the scouts' parents were catching up. "Now, listen carefully," said Gramps. "When I was a cub I used to play around that cave. Pretty scary place. We had a little rhyme we used to say.

"Giant Bat Cave
Of Beartown fame
Has the word 'giant'
In its name.
Giant Bat Cave . . .
Think about that.
Which is the giant,
The cave or the bat?"

The scouts looked at Gramps. What was he trying to tell them?

"Are you trying to tell us that there's some kind of giant monster bat living in that cave?" said Sister.

"Not tryin' to tell you anything," said Gramps. "Just sayin' a little rhyme we

used to say when we were cubs. Just
remember that last part:

> "Giant Bat Cave . . .
> Think about that.
> Which is the giant,
> The cave or *the bat*?"

Grizzly Gran caught up and took
Gramps by the arm. "Come on, Gramps.
You ought to be ashamed of yourself,
putting ideas into cubs' heads."

"Best place for ideas," said Gramps,
"inside cubs' heads." Gramps called back
over his shoulder. "Mind what I say, now.
Is it the cave that's giant? Or . . . is it the
bat?"

The scouts waited for their parents to
catch up. As they all headed home, the
Bear Scouts shared a single thought: If
there really were a giant monster bat in
Giant Bat Cave, Ralph's scheme would be
stopped in its tracks.

• Chapter 9 •
Visiting the Professor

The Bearsonian Institution looked like a
cross between a fortress and a castle. But
it wasn't either. It was a museum. It was
Bear Country's most important museum.
Its chief, Professor Actual Factual, was
Bear Country's most important scientist.

Actual Factual was the kind of scientist
who was interested in everything. He
studied plants and animals. He studied
the earth, the solar system, and the stars.
He was also the kind of scientist who went
to places and did things. He scuba-dived,
dug up dinosaur bones, rock-climbed, and

40

invented things. And all the while he was going and doing, *he was thinking*. That's the key to science: going, doing, and *thinking*.

The professor had helped the Bear Scouts many times before. They had high hopes that he would be able to help them with the problem of Giant Bat Cave.

But there was a sign hanging on the knob of the museum's door. In big letters it said, THE PROFESSOR IS OUT! In smaller letters it said, BE BACK SOON. Then in very small letters it said, WATCH THE SKIES.

What the heck did that mean?

"I think I can hear something," said Lizzy, who had extra-special good hearing. She said she could hear a mosquito a block away around the corner – and maybe she could.

Fred took off his glasses and looked up at the sky. Fred wore glasses because he was farsighted. That meant he could see things very far away.

"I think I see what Lizzy hears," he said. "It's not a bird. It's not exactly a plane. Why, it's Actual Factual!"

And sure enough it was.

BEARSONIAN
INSTITUTION

Professor Actual Factual landed right in front of the museum. "Happy to see you, my friends!" he shouted. "What do you think of my Miniplane? It's my latest invention!"

The scouts thought it was great. They crowded around the tiny plane. It looked almost like an easy chair with wings, a tail, and a motor.

"That's an old washing-machine motor. It worked very well," the professor said proudly. "There's only one problem. My washing machine doesn't work very well now."

"In any case, welcome!" said the professor. "My good friends the Bear Scouts are always welcome at the Bearsonian. And how is your lovely leader, Scout Leader Jane?"

"She's fine, Professor," said Brother as they walked through the museum's lobby. "But this isn't just a visit. We're here about a problem."

The Bear Scouts told Actual Factual the whole Giant Bat Cave story as he led them through the museum. They told him why they had gone to the big town hall meeting. They told him about Ralph's plan to turn Giant Bat Cave into an underground theme park. They told him about how they were worried about the bats that had lived in Giant Bat Cave for thousands of years.

The professor spoke not a word as they walked through the museum. They went through the Hall of Flight, where famous aircraft of Bear Country history were on view. They went through the Hall of Dinosaurs, where the great fossil skeletons were to be seen. Two prize skeletons were those of a Tyrannosaurus rex and a pteranodon, a large flying dinosaur. They went through the Hall of Energy, where the professor had built a huge Tesla Coil, which is a kind of lightning machine. The Bear Scouts had been to the museum many times before, of course. But every

time they came they were filled with the
wonder of science and nature.

Actual Factual unlocked the door of his
office and invited the Bear Scouts in. It
was an amazing place in its own right. It
was packed with books. There were blue-
prints tacked to the walls. There were

models of all kinds. There was a blackboard that was covered with numbers.

Actual Factual sat at his cluttered
desk. He had listened to the whole story
without saying a single word. The scouts
were beginning to wonder if he had been
listening.

"Well, Professor," said Brother. "What do
you think? We think it's serious."

Actual Factual got up and walked to
the blackboard. He rubbed out all the
numbers and wrote on the blackboard in
big bold letters:

OPERATION:
SAVE THE CAVE

• Chapter 10 •

Worse Than Serious

"It's worse than serious," he said. "It's an apocalypse!"

"Apoca-what?" said Sister.

"Definition, please," said the professor.

"*Apocalypse*: pronounced a-poc-a-lips," said Fred. "*Doom, total disaster.*"

"Thank you, Fred," said the professor. "But let me explain. In the first place, bats have lived in Giant Bat Cave not for thousands of years but for sixty million years. For that whole time they have been an important part of the balance of nature. What makes bats so important is that they eat lots of insects. Bats control insects better than anything else on earth."

"Better than birds?" said Brother.

"Better than frogs?" said Lizzy.

"Better than flyswatters?" said Sister.

"Better than all those put together," said the professor. "Bats eat tons and tons of insects."

"But, Professor," said Sister, "how could there be tons of anything as small as insects?"

"They make up in numbers what they lack in size," said the professor. He went to a globe in the corner of his office. "Just think about this. If you took all the land creatures on the earth and put them on one side of a scale, then you took all the insects of the earth and put them on the other side of the scale, the side with the insects would weigh more."

"Wow!" said the scouts.

"Now what does that say to you?" asked the professor.

"It says," said Sister, "that if we don't save the cave, we're all gonna get a lot more mosquito bites."

"That's one way of looking at it," said the professor. "Come, scouts. We've got things to attend to if we're going to save the cave."

"Where are we going?" asked Brother.

"When you have a problem," said the professor, "you go to its heart. In this case, the heart of the problem is Giant Bat Cave."

"Y-y-you mean we're going into Giant Bat Cave?" said Sister with a shiver.

"Have you ever been in there?" asked Fred nervously.

"Follow me, group," said Actual Factual. He led them out of his office and down a back stair. "Of course I have," said the professor. "Many, many times. It's an important study site. Why, I know Giant Bat Cave as well as I know the back of my paw." He stopped and looked at the back of his paw. "As a matter of fact, I may know Giant Bat Cave *better* than I know the back of my paw. But, be that as it may, we have places to go and things to do. This way, scouts!"

The back door opened on to the museum's car park. Actual Factual's famous Sciencemobile was parked there. It was a white van that Actual Factual had fitted out for science work. It had a telescope on

its roof. There were digging tools, ropes, and ladders hooked on to its sides. Inside was a mini laboratory with the chemicals needed to test water and air samples.

The scouts were excited. They had never ridden in the Sciencemobile. Now they were going to get their chance. But they were still a little nervous about where they were going. Maybe it was just a "study site" to the professor. But to the members of the Bear Scout troop, Giant Bat Cave was a pretty scary place. It was one they hadn't counted on visiting when they decided to try for the Good Government Merit Badge.

"This isn't the way!" said Fred when Actual Factual turned off the road into a swamp.

"It's a shortcut!" shouted the professor. "But don't worry. I know the swamp well."

The scouts held on tight as the Sciencemobile rocked and rolled through the muddy swamp.

• Chapter 11 •

HELLO! Hello! Hello!

"Here we are!" shouted the professor. He leaped out of the van and opened the back. He took out a special torch. It was hooked to a power pack that Actual Factual slipped on to his back.

The scouts were slow getting out of the van. They stared at the cave's jagged mouth. It looked even scarier in real life than it had looked on Ralph's slide.

The professor had gone over to look at a sign that had been put up in front of the cave. "Goodness!" he said. "This is much more serious than I thought." As the scouts joined him, Actual Factual read the sign aloud.

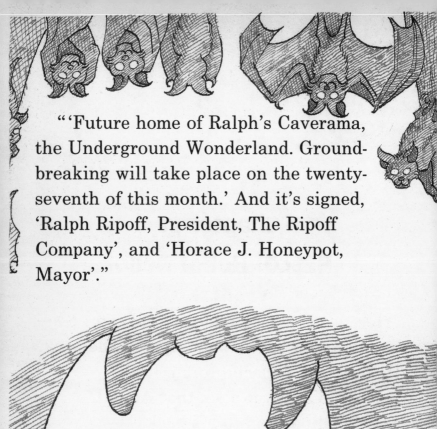

"'Future home of Ralph's Caverama, the Underground Wonderland. Ground-breaking will take place on the twenty-seventh of this month.' And it's signed, 'Ralph Ripoff, President, The Ripoff Company', and 'Horace J. Honeypot, Mayor'."

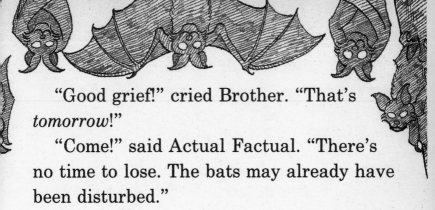

"Good grief!" cried Brother. "That's *tomorrow*!"

"Come!" said Actual Factual. "There's no time to lose. The bats may already have been disturbed."

Actual Factual walked into the cave as if he were walking into his own living room. The scouts followed along behind.

The scouts were nervous. Except for Lizzy, who was more worried about the bats than she was about being scared.

The cave mouth was big enough to drive a truck through. The inside of the cave was even bigger. "Wow!" said Fred. "You could park the Goodbear Airship in here and it wouldn't even touch the walls!"

Actual Factual turned on the big torch. It was very powerful. It cut through the gloom and placed a big circle of light on the roof of the cave. "Good," he said. "The bats look fine. They don't seem to have been disturbed at all."

"Bats?" said Fred, looking up. "I don't see any bats."

The roof of the cave looked like it was lined with black velvet. What the scouts didn't know was that the "black velvet" was thousands of bats hanging upside down.

The professor took some folding binoculars from his pocket. He told the scouts to have a closer look at the roof of

56

the cave. One by one the scouts looked up through the binoculars. They were amazed to see the bats, shoulder to shoulder, sound asleep.

"Aren't they beautiful?" said Lizzy.

"Well," said Sister, "I wouldn't exactly say that."

The torchlight was beginning to wake up some of the bats. The professor turned it off. That sent the cave back into a gloomy darkness. But after a while the Bear Scouts' eyes got used to the darkness and they could see the cave's sharp "teeth".

"Stalactites and stalagmites," said Brother softly.

"Which are which?" asked Sister.

"Here's a little rhyme to help you remember," said the professor.

"Stalactites and stalagmites,
Only caves have got 'em;
'Tites are always up on top,
'Mites are on the bottom."

The professor's rhyme might help them remember which was which. But it also reminded them of Grizzly Grampa's rhyme and got them a little scared again. It was easy to be scared in a place like Giant Bat Cave. It was like a different world. Even the sound was different. Caves are the home of echoes. So the professor wasn't surprised when the scouts started to try some out.

"HELLO!" they shouted, and it came back "Hello! Hello!"

"Please, friends," said Actual Factual. "It's not good manners to come into someone's home shouting at the top of our lungs. Especially the home of bats, who have such good hearing. That's how they catch insects. Flying insects make sound

waves. Bats hear them and catch them in mid-air."

"I expect that's why, when you see bats just before dark, they fly sort of zigzag?" said Fred.

"Yeah," said Sister, who remembered watching bats at twilight. "Sort of like dot to dot. Only the dots are bugs."

"Insects, if you please," said Actual Factual. "But we must not tarry. Come! On with the spelunk!"

"Spelunk?" said Sister.

"*Spelunk*," said Fred. "*To explore caves. Also, spelunking: the sport of exploring caves.*"

The professor had charged ahead into the cave. The scouts had to hurry to catch up.

• Chapter 12 •

A Different World

The professor really did seem to know
Giant Bat Cave like the back of his paw.
The scouts followed him into a narrow
tunnel. It was getting very dark.

"What's that sound up ahead?" said
Lizzy.

"It sounds like running water," said
Brother.

A fast-running underground river lay
just ahead in the darkness.

"How about your torch, Professor?" said
Brother.

"It's much too bright for this part of our
spelunk. Besides, we won't need it. My

new invention, the Handy Dandy Spelunka-boat, will be much better for this part of our trip."

That's the way it was with the professor. He always seemed to have a new invention up his sleeve. Only this one wasn't up his sleeve. It was in a hiding place in the cave tunnel. It was hard to make it out in the dark. But the cubs would see it soon enough.

The professor pressed a button. There was a loud hissing sound. Before you could say Handy Dandy Spelunka-boat, the scouts were looking at an amazing boat that glowed like a light bulb.

"It's nothing, really," said the professor. "I just combined the idea of the self-inflating rubber raft with clear plastic and a gas that glows in the dark."

He pushed the glowing boat into the river and held it while the scouts piled in. He started the motor, and just like that, Professor Actual Factual and the Bear Scouts were putt-putting down the underground river in a boat that glowed like a light bulb. It lit not only the tunnel above but the water below.

"Look!" cried Scout Lizzy. "Fish! Lots and lots of them!"

"I didn't know fish lived in caves," said Scout Sister.

"Of course they do," said Actual Factual as he steered their glowing boat along the winding underground waterway. "All sorts of flora and fauna live in caves."

"Hit it, Fred," said Sister.

"*Flora,*" said Fred. "*Plants or plant life. Fauna. Animals or animal life.*"

The river tunnel had opened up into a great underground room. It had a wide, curved ceiling. There were huge stone pillars made of stalactites and stalagmites that had grown together. It was almost like a palace ballroom. Only instead of a polished floor to dance upon, there was smooth water to float upon.

The only sound was the putt-putt of the motor as the glowing boat steered among the great pillars of stone. The Bear Scouts looked around in wonder as Actual Factual steered for a tunnel at the far end of the room.

"The river tunnel had opened
up into a great underground room."

• Chapter 13 •

Daylight Ahead!

"Look!" cried Brother. "Daylight ahead!"

"No," said the professor, with a smile.
"It's the light of the most amazing of all
forms of cave life: *Lampyrus noctuluca*,
better known as 'glowworm'."

The scouts hardly breathed as they
passed through a tunnel lit by the bodies
of thousands of glowing worms.

A few more twists and turns, and there
really was daylight ahead. It was another
cave entrance – a secret one that only
Actual Factual knew about. He steered the
boat on to a rocky beach that was littered
with stalactites that had broken off and

68

fallen. Actual Factual and the scouts
pressed the gas out of the boat. Then they
rolled it up and put it in another of the
professor's hiding places.

The spelunk had been quite an experi-
ence. Nobody had spoken for a long time.
It was Brother who broke the silence.

"Professor," he said, "there's no question
about it. We simply must save this cave.
Ralph Ripoff doesn't have to make it into
an underground wonderland. It already is
an underground wonderland. An absolute-
ly amazing underground wonderland. It
must be protected. Will you help us,
Professor?"

"With all my heart," said the professor.
"What do you want me to do?"

"Come with us to see the mayor. Today!
Right now! We're just cubs. But you're a
great scientist. Surely he'll listen to you."

"Then let's do it!" cried the professor.
He started to leave but stopped to watch
the scouts. They had picked up broken

ONE FOR ALL,
AND ALL FOR ONE!

stalactites. They were crossing them like swords and were about to say their slogan.

The professor picked up a stalactite and joined them. Their shout of "One for all, and all for one!" echoed and re-echoed through the cave.

The professor climbed out of the cave with the Bear Scouts close behind.

• Chapter 14 •

A Meeting with the Mayor

"You may see the mayor now," said the mayor's secretary.

The mayor's office was very important looking. It had important-looking furniture, and there were important-looking paintings on the wall. Mayor Horace J. Honeypot himself was sitting behind an important-looking desk. Standing behind the mayor was Ralph Ripoff.

"Professor Actual! I wid you belcome – er, bid you welcome!" said the mayor with a big smile.

But when Ralph leaned forward and whispered something in the mayor's ear,

71

his smile turned into a frown. "Those bubs – er, cubs – with you," said the mayor, "are the bubs – er, cubs – who made a big fuss at the town meeting!"

"It is because of these bubs – er, cubs – that I am here," said the professor. "Mr Mayor, you must not go ahead with your plan to destroy that wonder of nature known as Giant Bat Cave!"

"We're not going to destroy it, my fear dellow – er, dear fellow," said the mayor. "We're going to *improve* it."

"That's right," said Ralph. "We're going to turn that worthless hole in the ground into the greatest thing since ice-cream came with chocolate flakes. What's the matter with you, Professor? Are you against progress?"

"I am very much *for* progress, sir," said Actual Factual. "But change is not always progress."

"And what's going to happen to the bats?" said Lizzy.

"And the *Lampy* . . . *Lampy* . . . the glowworms?" said Sister.

"And the stalactites and stalagmites?" said Fred.

"That's all taken care of," said Ralph. "The mayor has already hired another one of my companies, Ripoff Exterminators, to take care of the bats and all that other cave rubbish. We're going to seal the cave off and gas it. Then we're going to bulldoze the whole mess into the swamp."

"Oh, dear! Oh, dear!" said Professor Actual Factual. "You can't do that. It would hurt the ecology of the whole—"

"Ecology doesn't pay the bills, Professor," said Ralph. He reached over to the mayor's desk and grabbed a fistful of papers. "Contracts, cheques, and deals is what pays the bills. Cash, moolah, the long green!"

"Moolah? Long green?" said the professor. "I don't understand."

"It means money, Professor," said Brother.

"Now, if you'll excuse us, Professor," said the mayor, "Mr Dipoff – er, Ripoff – and I have things to do."

Actual Factual and the scouts turned to leave.

"Just a minute, Professor," said Ralph. "Do you know anything about this?" He took something from his pocket. It was a piece of paper. He unfolded it. He held it up for all to see. This is what it looked like:

Giant Bat Cave
of Beartown Fame
Has the word "giant"
In its name.
Giant Bat Cave...
Think about that.
Which is the giant,
The cave or the bat?
Beware the
VAMPIRE!!!

"The mayor found this nailed to his office door this morning," said Ralph.

"Humph!" said the mayor. "The very idea of a giant bampire vat – er, vampire bat – living in that cave. It's p-p-pure piffle! Sh-sh-sheer cockypop – er, poppycock!"

"And l-l-let me tell you this," said Ralph in an even shakier voice than the mayor's. "If you or anybody else thinks they can scare us off, they've got another think coming! V-v-vampire bat, indeed!"

"What nonsense," said the professor. "Come on, scouts. We are wasting our time here."

• Chapter 15 •

The Seed of Fear

The professor and the scouts were looking gloomy as they left the mayor's office. Except for Brother. He had that deep-in-thought look that meant he might be getting an idea.

"Professor," he said, "I don't think we were wasting our time back there. I noticed something that could be important. Ralph and the mayor were a lot more worried about a giant vampire bat than they were about the ecology of the planet."

"Brother's right," said Fred. "They were sweating and shaking when they talked about it."

"A giant monster vampire bat," snorted the professor. "Pure piffle. Or as our esteemed mayor said, sheer cockypop – er, poppycock."

They were walking to where the Sciencemobile was parked.

"Maybe so, Professor," said Brother, "but look at it this way. *You* know that vampires are poppycock. And *we* know that vampires are poppycock. But it looked to me like Ralph and the mayor aren't so sure vampires are poppycock. You saw how they were sweating and shaking about that warning Gramps nailed to the mayor's door."

"Your grandfather did that?" said the professor in a shocked voice.

"Of course," said Brother. "He thinks the only way we're going to save the cave is to beat Ralph at his own game – to trick him, to scare him off. And I think he may be right!"

"What are you saying?" said the professor.

"I'm saying Gramps planted the seed of fear. Now it's up to us to water it and help it grow until . . ."

The professor got the message. He finished Brother's sentence. " . . . until it grows into a giant monster vampire bat that will scare certain bears so much that they'll never go near Giant Bat Cave as long as they live!"

"Do you think you can do it?" asked Brother.

The professor didn't answer. The Bear Scouts could almost feel Actual Factual's mighty brain powering up for the job of creating a giant monster vampire bat.

"Be at the museum first thing in the morning," said the professor. "Come around to the back door."

The scouts watched as he climbed into the Sciencemobile and drove away. They headed home.

• Chapter 16 •
Not a Second to Lose

The Bear Scouts got to the museum
bright and early the next morning. But
when they went around to the back door,
they saw that Grizzly Gramps had got
there brighter and earlier. At least that
looked like Gramps's pickup truck parked
beside Actual Factual's Sciencemobile.

The scouts went in the back door. Beyond it there was a second door that had a sign on it. The sign said, OPERATION: SAVE THE CAVE – KNOCK BEFORE ENTERING. Grizzly Gramps let them in.

"What are you doing here, Gramps?" asked Brother.

"Shh!" said Gramps. "The professor's been working around the clock and he's hit a rough spot. He called me last night. Said he was going to need my truck for Operation: Save the Cave. So here I am."

The room they were in was Actual Factual's secret workshop. It was the place where he worked on his inventions. There were half-finished inventions around the room. But his latest invention, the one that was supposed to scare Ralph and the mayor out of their wits and save the cave, didn't seem to be going well. There were parts spread all over the floor. Some of the parts looked as if they came from the professor's miniplane.

"What sort of a rough spot?" asked Fred.

The professor was over at the other side of the room, working at his computer.

"It's a little over my head," said Gramps. "As nearly as I can tell, he's havin' trouble findin' the right wing shape for Vee-Bee-One."

"Vee-Bee-One?" said Sister.

"Code name for Vampire Bat One," said Gramps. "I figured a bat wing ought to work. But the professor says no."

Fred looked at the mess of parts spread all over the floor. "Wow," he said. "That looks like something somebody took apart and couldn't put back together again."

The scouts went over to where the professor was busily tapping away at his computer. As he tapped, pictures of different kinds of wings showed on the screen. A gull wing, a robin wing, a dragonfly wing. Wing after wing after wing.

"Why not a bat wing?" asked Fred.

"Bats, also birds and insects, fly by flapping their wings. The flapping problem is famous. No inventor has ever solved it. Except for Mother Nature, of course, who is the greatest inventor of them all."

He kept on tapping, calling up one wing after another. Suddenly he leaped up with a startled cry. "Eureka!" he shouted. His chair went over backwards with him in it.

"Fred," said Sister, snapping her fingers.

"*Eureka*," said Fred. "*Cry of joy at the moment of discovery.*"

"Of course!" said the professor as the scouts helped him up. "The pteranodon wing! Pteranodon could flap, but mostly it was a glider. Why didn't I think of it? We have a pteranodon fossil right here in the museum. It's the perfect wing for our purpose!"

The work went quickly after that. As they worked, Actual Factual filled them in on how Vampire Bat One was supposed to operate.

"'Supposed' being the key word," admitted the professor. "What I'm doing is combining my Miniplane with a helium-filled bat balloon."

"What's helium?" asked Sister.

"It's a gas," said the professor. "The kind they put in birthday balloons that fly away when you let go of the string." The professor went on working as he spoke. "Now, we'll set these little red Christmas tree lights in the head so that the eyes and mouth will glow."

"What are those shells?" asked Lizzy.

"Razor clam shells," said the professor. "They're very light and will make excellent fangs. All right, that does it! We're ready to go!"

"But, Professor," said Brother. "Aren't you going to inflate the bat balloon and put the whole thing together?"

"I wish we could," said the professor. "But it would be much too large to fit in the truck. Somebody would surely see it. Then the bat would be out of the bag. No, we're going to have to load the parts into the truck. Then go through the swamp to the secret cave entrance."

"Why not the main entrance?" asked Brother.

"Because there's a work crew there setting things up for Ralph and the mayor," said the professor. "So we're going to have to use the spelunka-boat to carry everything to the main cave."

"But, Professor," said Lizzy, "that'll take for ever!"

"No," said the professor, looking at his watch. "It will take us nine hours and twenty-two minutes, which means we'll have Vee-Bee-One put together in the main cave and ready to fly at sunset. Sunset is very important. First, because that's when Ralph and the mayor are supposed to show up. Two, that's when the thousands of bats will fly out of the cave for their evening meal. And three, because with the sun in their eyes, Ralph and the mayor will be more easily fooled. Now, let's move! There's not a second to lose, and we have a lot of hard work ahead of us!"

• Chapter 17 •

It's a Bird! It's a Plane!
It's a Vampire!

A *lot* of hard work. But by the time the
sun had turned red and begun to set,
everything was in place.

The scouts were hiding in the bushes at
the edge of the swamp. They would be on

the lookout for Ralph and the mayor. When they arrived, Lizzy would signal to Actual Factual with a whippoorwill bird call. Actual Factual would be inside the cave, ready to take off. Gramps was waiting in his truck in a meadow just beyond the swamp.

Then, if all went well, Actual Factual would fly over the swamp and land in the meadow. The scouts would make their way through the swamp over a safe path that Actual Factual had mapped out for them. They would all pitch in and take the vampire apart and load it into the truck. They would zip over to the secret cave entrance and pick up the Sciencemobile. Then they would scoot back to the museum before anyone was the wiser.

The mayor and Ralph arrived in the mayor's car just as the sun was setting. They were very pleased with the job that the work crew had done. The sound system was working and the grandstand was ready for guests who would be arriving later.

"Mr Mayor," said Ralph, "I think it's safe to say that you and I are about to make a killing. And I don't mean those crummy bats. I mean . . ."

"I know," said the mayor. "You mean mash, goolah – er, cash, moolah, the long green."

Neither Ralph nor the mayor noticed the call of a whippoorwill.

"And speaking of bats," said Ralph, "here come those crummy bats now and . . . AND THEY'VE GOT THEIR BIG BROTHER WITH THEM. THEIR *VERY* BIG BROTHER!"

"It's the vampire!" screamed the mayor. "Run for your life!"

Vampire Bat One flew right at them, its eyes and mouth aglow with red Christmas tree lights. Ralph and the mayor could almost feel the razor-clam-shell fangs on their necks.

"Into the swamp!" screamed Ralph.

Before you could say "oohey, gooey, phewy," Ralph and the mayor were shoulder-deep in the awful swamp mud.

That was the end of Ralph's Caverama. The invited guests didn't find Mayor Horace J. Honeypot and Ralph Ripoff, President of the Ripoff Company, when they arrived. They found two strange, mud-covered creatures babbling something about . . . a giant vampire bat?

It was very embarrassing for the mayor, but not for Ralph. It's not easy to embarrass a crook like Ralph.

• Chapter 18 •

It's Pretty Hard to Impress a Chicken

A few days later the Bear Scouts were relaxing in their secret clubhouse. They were proud of themselves. They had a right to be. They had not only helped save the cave, they had earned not one but three merit badges. That's right, three.

Professor Actual Factual lost no time telling his friend, Scout Leader Jane, the whole story of the saving of Giant Bat Cave. Now the scouts had three new merit badges to add to their honour wall: the Good Government Merit Badge, the Ecology Merit Badge, *and* the Spelunking Merit Badge.

Surely this was a time to say their slogan.
They looked around their clubhouse. There
was nothing to cross.

"Fingers," said Sister.

That's what they did. They crossed fingers
and shouted, "One for all, and all for one!"

Even the chicken who had wandered in was impressed. And everyone knows how hard it is to impress a chicken.

**Don't miss
THE
Berestain
BEAR
SCOUTS
And The
Humongous Pumpkin**

Pretty soon Sister began to have a
dream. But let's not mince words. Sister
began to have a galloping rip-roaring
nightmare! It wasn't the spooky pumpkins
she dreamed about, the witch, the monster, or the vampire. It was the pumpkins'
insides she dreamed about – those wet,
gloppy, seedy insides. In the dream they
rose up out of the bucket and formed into
a wet gloppy weasel. A giant wet gloppy
weasel. As soon as it formed, it began to
chase Sister. She ran as fast as her legs

could carry her. But the weasel monster kept getting closer and closer. The monster was just about to get her when she tripped over some kind of giant root and woke up.

But it turned out not only that the giant root was real, it was a giant *pumpkin* root. It had grown under her sleeping bag and lifted her up in the air. And it was still growing! That wasn't all that was still growing. Sister couldn't believe her eyes when she saw it. It was a humongous pumpkin. It was already as big as a house and it was still growing.

I must still be dreaming, thought Sister, but *maybe not!*

YOUNG HIPPO FUNNY

Have a giggle with a Young Hippo Funny!

Bod's Mum's Knickers
Bod's Mum has some ENORMOUS and very
useful knickers!
Peter Beere

Metal Muncher
Life's not easy when your baby brother likes to ... *eat metal* !
Kathy Henderson

Count Draco Down Under
Stacey has a strange new visitor – he's a VAMPIRE!
Ann Jungman

Emily H and the Enormous Tarantula
Emily H and the Stranger in the Castle
Emily H Turns Detective
Three funny books about Emily H and her special pet –
Theo, the world's most enormous TARANTULA!
Kara May

Professor Blabbermouth on the Moon
Tonight's the night for Operation Moon Cheese!
Nigel Watts

YOUNG HiPPO MAGIC

Anything is possible in these enchanting stories from
Young Hippo Magic!

My Friend's a Gris-Quok!
Alex has a deep, dark secret. He's half Gris-Quok!
Malorie Blackman

Diggory and the Boa Conductor
Why do MAGICAL things happen to ordinary Diggory?

The Little Pet Dragon
James's puppy is glimmering with magic!
Philippa Gregory

Broomstick Services
One day Joe, Lucy and Jackie find *three witches*!
Ann Jungman

The Marmalade Pony
Hannah has always longed for her very own pony...
Linda Newbery

Mr Wellington Boots
Watch out - there's a MAGICAL CAT about!
Ann Ruffell

The Wishing Horse
Albert the horse grants *very* special wishes...
Malcolm Yorke

YOUNG HiPPO SCHOOL

Something exciting is always happening at school in the
Young Hippo School series!

Off to School
Lisa, Ben and Max discover runaway buses, the Big Shirt
Race and a Santa who *takes* presents away!
Jean Chapman

Class Four's Wild Week
Mr Player can't keep up with his class – not because they're
naughty, but because they're too CLEVER!
Malcolm Yorke

Nightingale News
Read all about Jack, Chantelle, Melodie, Owen and
Mustapha's hidden talents!
Odette Elliott

The Grott Street Gang
Something HUGE, hairy and *banana-eating* is about to help
The Grott Street Gang with a dastardly dangerous deed!
Terry Deary